The Inn at Willow Creek

By

Beverly Miller

Enjoy!

Beverly Miller
2003

ISBN: 1-4107-4420-5 (e-book)
ISBN: 1-4107-4421-3 (Paperback)
ISBN: 1-4107-4422-1 (Dust Jacket)

This book is printed on acid free paper.

1stBooks – rev. 06/12/03

Prologue

"If you think you're going to waltz in here and move Jake and Annie to some nursing home, it will be over my dead body!" she told him, as she poked her finger into his chest.

Small droplets of rain trickled down her face from the wet tangle of mahogany colored curls piled high on her head. She was angry and her dark eyes shot sparks at him as she waited for his reply.

Who is this lunatic, he wondered? She had surprised him and Timothy J. McConnell, hated surprises.

Timothy J. McConnell was Scotch/Irish and proud of it with copper blonde hair and soft green eyes to prove it, stubborn, impatient, hot-tempered and somewhat arrogant.

Timothy J. McConnell; heart breaker, wealth seeker, real estate broker, known to drink green beer with the best of them on St. Pattie's Day, kind to old ladies and small fuzzy dogs.

Chapter 1

Low dark clouds made that late March day gray and depressing, almost as if the world was suddenly without color. An endless mist kept the windshield wipers moving at that slow hypnotizing pace.

He'd been on the road since dawn and even the blare of "KWPX – Radio for the 90's" couldn't keep Tim's attention. He tried everything, opening the window, adjusting the seat, taking another sip of the bitter cold coffee from the truck stop a hundred miles back. Interstate 70 had become monotonous, stretching out ahead of him, a gray flat ribbon as far as the eye could see. *Maybe I should have brought Ellen along for company*, he thought. *No, that would have been a mistake.*

Tim had divided all cars and women into two distinct categories; high and low maintenance. Ellen had started out on the low side of the scale, but was rapidly working her way up. Everything in her life seemed to be a catastrophic event. Her car wouldn't start, her mother hadn't called, her law professor didn't like her. She called Tim constantly, wanting him to solve all her problems.

But when a woman became too needy, Tim always backed away. Money was his first priority and Ellen was beginning to irritate him. "Can't you make a decision without involving me?" Tim had asked the night before.

"Sure I can!" she stated, as she slammed the receiver down.

.

1

Her anger had been short lived, however, and she had called him again this morning before he was out of the city limits. She had passed her bar exam, but couldn't decide which firm to join. She had two job offers, both with excellent law firms and she'd been struggling with her decision for weeks now, always wanting Tim to decide for her.

"I can't help you with this, Ellen. It has to be your decision."

No, he was glad he hadn't brought her along today. He needed to be away to think, to decide if she was really that important to him. Ellen was bright, talented, sexy, all the things he thought he wanted. But, sometimes she was so insecure. Tim was beginning to feel like her therapist.

A semi suddenly whirled past, waking Tim from his thoughts. It sprayed water out across the hood and onto the windshield. The rain was getting heavier now and he needed to pay more attention to the road. He glanced across at the map in the seat next to him, hurriedly changed lanes and left the interstate behind.

Tim turned his little 1960 Corvette onto a country road, where the terrain changed from flat farm ground to rolling hills and trees. The sharp curves and ever-narrowing highway made him sit up and take notice. The hills rolled on, and thirty minutes went by without meeting another car. He went by several farms and ranches then around a curve and into the woods again. Finally, at a remote intersection, stood an old country store and feed mill. The sign read, "Martin's Mercantile".

Where am I, Mayberry, he wondered? He wasn't sure which way to turn, but didn't stop to ask directions.

He pulled over and looked at his map, but this particular road wasn't on it, only a small red dot that his father had circled. He wandered on, hoping to see something that might indicate the whereabouts of the family estate.

At age 32, Timothy J. McConnell was on his way to confront his great-uncle and aunt with the idea of moving them into a retirement home in the nearby town of Blakesburg, Missouri. After a report from their doctor had reached Tim's family in Chicago, he convinced himself and his parents that moving the old couple out of the family estate would be the best for everyone. The report had stated that both Jacob, age 84, and Annebelle McConnell, age 82, were in failing health and shouldn't spend another winter alone in the country house.

Jacob's diabetes was worsening and his medication needed supervision. Annebelle was developing a heart condition and neither of them had been eating right. Their age was taking its toll and with no children of their own, Dr. Davis had decided to contact their only living relatives.

His letter went on to say:

I feel the responsibility of the McConnells' care can no longer be left to the generosity of their neighbors and friends. Please contact my office if you have any questions regarding this matter.

Respectfully,
Dr. Charles Davis, MD

Neither Tim nor his parents had ever met Jacob or Annebelle, but the doctor's letter brought back mental images of old-fashioned elegance and wealth that Tim's grandfather had talked about so lovingly.

This could be the perfect opportunity to liquidate those family assets, Tim thought. It hadn't been difficult for him to convince his father, a successful stockbroker, that selling the estate and investing the money was the best answer. *Jacob and Annebelle will probably be much better off in town, anyway. This deal will be quick and clean and to everyone's advantage.*

Tim had offered to take a few days off, go to Missouri, move the elderly couple to town and sell off the homestead and its contents. After all, he had lots of experience in real estate, some good and some not so good.

He'd been putting together a deal on a large commercial complex for the past six months. He was anxious to close; too anxious. He pushed the buyer, making too many demands, pushing, always pushing. The buyer backed out and everything fell through. Six months of hard work and a $200,000 commission was gone.

Patience wasn't one of Tim's virtues. He would move old Jacob and Annebelle and then concentrate on selling their properties. *This will be a breeze compared to what I've been going through*, he thought to himself. *If Uncle Jacob's estate is half as wonderful as I think, there will be no problem selling it.*

Tim's Grandfather McConnell had told of a grand and beautiful brick home, surrounded by woods, and pastures filled with cattle and horses. The estate had been visited by guests from all over the world. They had dined and danced in the lap of luxury, tended to by servants in starched uniforms.

The family money had come from cattle. Tim's great-great grandfather, Jonathan McConnell, had come from the east coast by wagon to Missouri with a pair of purebred Angus calves. From their union, Jonathan eventually acquired the finest herd of cattle west of Scotland. In time, heads of state from China, Europe and South America heard about this vigorous new breed, sturdy, healthy and heavy with tender beef. Many came to see for themselves. Others sent for the McConnells to come to take orders and ship the cattle overseas. Beside cattle orders, they acquired rare and beautiful treasures from around the world.

Along with notoriety came wealth and power. There was power in local and national decisions, with enough money to make things happen. By 1880, Jonathan and his son had acquired as much as 2,000 acres of woods and rich pasture, along with some of the most beautiful land in America.

Through the years, more and more additions were added to the original house. The estate had become a landmark, built for entertaining and business. Jonathan McConnell was a master at both. He could dine with politicians, make a cattle deal and explain how to make wine, all at the same time.

The Missouri area had become well-known and respected for its cattle. The railroad came through their property and became the best way to ship the livestock. The McConnells bought interest in the railroad. The great limestone cliffs near the river meant quarries and the McConnells bought in. Local German settlers in the area brought grapevines from the glorious Rhineland. They started vineyards and used the limestone caves nearby as wineries, and the McConnells bought in. Lumber was needed for homes in St. Louis and Kansas City. The McConnells cut timber and started their own saw mill. Now they could ship lumber and cattle on the same train, their train.

Horses and mules had been in great demand, especially by the U.S. Army. So, the McConnells raised the very best and sold them at high profits. They had it all: money, power, respect.

But, over time, the empire was handed down from generation to generation. Each time there was a changing of the guard, less time was spent making money and more time consuming it.

Now, as Tim drove down the winding road, he remembered more of the old stories about his family's wealth and fame. He was getting anxious now to see this magnificent estate. It would be a realtor's dream. Not only would he make a huge commission, he would someday inherit most of the earnings from the sale. It was a real win-win situation.

An old weather-beaten mailbox, by the side of the road, gave Tim notice that the estate was near. In hand-painted letters it read, "J.J. McConnell". Around the next bend, he saw it.

It wasn't at all as he had pictured it. Soggy dead leaves blanketed the ground like old wet newspapers. Along the edge of the woods stood a desolate old house, badly in need of repair. The barns and outbuildings were nearly obscured by weeds and brush. A few head of cattle grazed along the creek beyond the barn, mired in mud. Fog hung low over the pond in front of the house and miles of wooden fences that lined the drive, hung dilapidated and broken.

Childhood images of a magnificent family estate were giving way now to a bitter dose of reality. With a heavy heart, Tim slowly turned into the drive and squirmed up the muddy path to the house.

The place seemed deserted, but he stepped out of his car and into the mist. It had been a long drive and this <u>had</u> to be the wrong place. He decided to go back down the road to the little store on the corner, to find out where the McConnell estate was.

Just then, a dim slice of light appeared, as the tall oak doors opened and out marched a young lady, flushed with anger. "Before you go in, I want a word with you," she said as she grabbed his arm and pulled him away from the house.

"I'm not sure I'm at the right place," Tim stated. "I'm looking for the McConnells."

"Oh, you're at the right place alright! If you think you're going to waltz in here and move Jake and Annie to some nursing home, it will be over my dead body!" she told him, as she poked her finger into his chest.

Small droplets of rain trickled down her face from the wet tangle of mahogany colored curls piled high on her head. She was angry and her dark eyes shot sparks at him as she waited for his reply.

Who is this lunatic, he wondered? She had surprised him and Timothy J. McConnell hated surprises.

"Do you think you can come in here and kick them out of their own home? You McConnells haven't cared about them or this place until now. I'm their neighbor, Jenna Adams, and I'm telling you to go back to Chicago where you belong!"

"Miss Adams, is it? There's no need to get on a high horse with me. Dr. Davis notified my family that Jacob and Annebelle were not well. I've only come to see about their health and well-being."

"'Their health and well-being' my eye! You've come to sell off everything they've got and warehouse them in some nursing home. I've heard all about Timothy McConnell, real estate whiz. What's the matter, can't you get the rich and famous for clients anymore? Now you want to sell off the only thing on earth that Jake and Annie have to live for?

"But, Dr. Davis tells us that…"

"Dr. Davis, Dr. Davis," Jenna interrupted. "All Chuck wants is for me to spend more time with him and less time here."

"Jenna!" shouted a man from the doorway, "bring our guest in from the rain. We'll speak of these matters after dinner." The frail old man motioned for them to come in. "Hello, young Timothy. We've been expecting you", he said with a slight Irish brogue.

"Don't let Jenna scare you, she means well." Jenna rolled her eyes at that remark.

Tim walked up to the man and held out his hand, "Uncle Jacob, I'm so glad to meet you at last. I've wanted to come here since I was a kid."

"Then, why didn't you?" asked Jenna under her breath, as she brushed past them and disappeared down the hallway.

"Is she always like that?"

"She'll grow on you," Jake laughed. "She's very protective of us and loves this place almost as much as we do."

Well, Tim thought, *that's interesting. Maybe she's my new buyer. I wonder if she could come up with some hard cash?*

"Come along, Timothy, and meet my little Annie." Jacob McConnell held his shoulders back and led the way through the large entry hall, past the huge, winding stairway and into the kitchen. Tim noticed only one bare light bulb in the entire hall. The house was cold and damp. Heavy draperies covered the windows in the rooms along the hall, making them dark and eerie. The walls were paneled in oak and lined with long dusty tapestries and heavy mirrors in ornate gold frames. Large nude statues stood like soldiers all along the hallway. Tim felt them watching, judging his intentions as he walked past.

In the kitchen they found an elderly woman with Jenna, peeling potatoes at an old metal sink. She was tiny and hunched over, her gray hair squirting out in every direction from the bun in the back. She wore an old blue housedress that looked as if she'd been caught in the 50's.

9

Tim looked around the kitchen and could see why. A yellowed, old refrigerator stood in one corner. The dinette set was red with chrome legs and Tim was sure "Ozzie and Harriet" must have had one just like it. A green enameled gas stove, piled high with pots, sat along one wall. The cupboards went up to the ceiling, taking a ladder to put anything in them. Each one had a glass door that allowed the clutter inside to show. Three or four of the doors were covered with yellow contact paper and Tim was afraid to imagine what might be behind those. Dishes were everywhere, and the countertop couldn't possibly hold one more item. *Do I really want to eat here,* he wondered?

Jake tapped Annie on the shoulder. "Dear, this is Timothy, James' son, you know, from Chicago."

Annie turned around. She looked at Tim, then down at the floor. "Hello."

Tim took her little hand. "It's nice to meet you, Aunt Annebelle." He went to sit down but there were stacks of old newspapers on each chair. No one offered to move them, so after an awkward moment, Tim picked up a stack and set it on the floor. A scrounge of a dog lay on an old rug near the back door. Tim thought he saw it breathe once, other than that, it never moved.

"Timothy and I are hungry, ladies. What's for dinner?" Jake asked as he picked up his knife and fork.

"It'll be awhile. The potatoes aren't even on to cook yet. I guess I left my post. Sorry, Annie," Jenna said as she hugged her tiny friend.

"Please don't go to any trouble on my account."

"Well, when someone comes unannounced, it's always trouble," Jenna snapped back. "If I hadn't stopped at the clinic after work today, we wouldn't have known you were coming at all. Dear, concerned Dr. Davis mentioned that your father called, wondering if you arrived safely. He said you were planning to stay here at the house for awhile. So thoughtful of you to let us know," sarcasm dripping from every word.

"I don't want to stay here if it's an inconvenience. I can just go to a hotel," Tim stammered with embarrassment. "I only thought with all of these rooms, maybe I could stay here and get acquainted."

"With us or with the house?" Jenna wasn't going to make this easy for him.

"Now, now, we have plenty of room, especially for family. It's just that we're not used to company. Jenna looks in on us each day and sometimes she spends the night if we're not feeling well. Otherwise, we don't see many folks these days. No one thinks I can drive anymore," Jake added sadly. "Years ago we put up twenty or more people every weekend. My mother always had us all dress for dinner. Oh, she was a beauty. This house was filled with food, friends and lots of laughter." Annie turned and gave him a tired, forlorn look that told Tim this place hadn't been filled with food, friends or laughter in many, many years.

Quietly Annie said, "Your mother had servants."

Jake never heard her. He was back in a world of parties and famous people. He rattled on for twenty minutes or more, telling tales

Beverly Miller

of old glory days when the McConnells owned half the county, as far as the eye could see. He told of senators and ambassadors. He knew their names, their wives' names, their children, the year they came, how long they stayed and what they ate. It was like listening to an old diary, written years ago.

The warmth from the kitchen fireplace, the dingy lighting, the long trip and the drone of Jake's voice was putting Tim to sleep. His mind must have wondered off for a moment. "Can't you see he's not one bit interested in the family history or this place, Jake? He could care less." Jenna's voice jolted Tim back into reality.

Next to eating glass, he couldn't think of anything he'd rather do than spend the next few days here. It wasn't going to be easy. Something was going on between Jenna and Dr. Davis, you could feel it every time his name was mentioned. Tim would have to wait to talk to Jake and Annie about moving, when they were alone. Jenna was too hostile.

The four of them sat at the chrome dinette set, each with a tiny piece of beef, a boiled potato and a slice of bread, no butter. The diet Tim had been contemplating might become a reality.

He was about to ask why the water tasted so strange, when Jake announced, "All the water for the house is held in a tank on the roof. It holds hundreds of gallons. It works like a water tower, giving constant pressure, no need for a pump to run," Jake explained proudly. "It probably takes six or eight months for me and Annie to use that much water." That explained it! Eight months with the same water in a rusty tank on top of the house. *Oh, the algae.* Tim didn't know whether to swallow or spit. *I should have had my shots updated.*

Just then, someone knocked loudly on the back door. Jenna jumped up to answer it. A short, pudgy old man peered in through the door, his gray hooded sweatshirt tied tight around his face. He was soaking wet and he hurriedly stepped inside as a clap of thunder startled him.

"Hey, Teddy. What's up?"

"Oh, Jenna. I'm so glad yer still here. I need yer help! Three calves were born today and I can only find one of 'em. They're out in the pasture, it's rainin' buckets, and the creek's almost outta her banks. If we don't find 'em soon, they'll drown," Teddy yelled above the storm.

"Okay, we'll be right there!" Jenna flew past the table then stopped. "Don't just sit there, McConnell, let's go!"

Jenna Adams has high maintenance written all over her, Tim thought to himself. *Why am I letting her intimidate me?* He didn't usually let women talk to him in that tone of voice, but he got up and followed her as if he actually knew where he was going. They went into the cellar. Out from under the steps, she threw him a pair of hip boots, a yellow slicker, an old fishing hat complete with flies and lures attached, and two brown leather gloves for the same hand. Lord only knew what might be growing in those boots. While he anticipated putting them on, Jenna dressed in orange coveralls and boots. As she tied an old plastic rain bonnet over her hair, she yelled at him to hurry up.

Tim was 6'2" tall and weighed in around 200 pounds, but everything he had on was too big. As he clomped his way up the cellar steps, Jake stated, "Theodore Roosevelt wore hip boots like those to fish in that very stream. What year was that Annie?"

The hooks dug into Tim's head as he hurried out the door to join Jenna. He pictured himself as the poster child for the "Isaac Walton League" and could only imagine what he must look like in this get-up.

They scrambled into Teddy's rusty old Ford pickup. There was a nasty-looking gear shift in the middle, so Jenna was forced to sit on Tim's lap. "I'm not sitting here. I'd rather be in the back."

Tim opened the door, "Good!" he announced, as he deposited her onto the ground with a splat. She rode alone on the tailgate in the rain, all the way to the creek.

Teddy jumped out and quickly lit three lanterns. It was raining much harder now, and they could hear the roar of the water flowing in the creek.

Jenna held her lantern up to Tim's face, "Have you ever been around animals?"

"Sure!" Tim answered, thinking of the time he flushed his dead goldfish. He certainly wasn't going to admit that the only beef he'd ever been around was on a plate marked "Medium-Rare." *I'm an heir to the McConnell Cattle Empire, therefore I must know something,* he decided.

Teddy went north and Tim and Jenna went south. It was like walking on a wet sponge. The ground was so saturated, there was nowhere for the water to go.

The creek was starting to spill out over the bank. A little farther down stream was a big clump of willows. Jenna searched the tall grass, pushing it back with her boots. The driving rain made it extremely hard to see. Tim followed her, trying to keep the mud from sucking off his boots.

There in the brush lay a new little calf. Jenna tried to get it on its feet, but it was too weak to stand. "Help me!" she yelled.

Tim put down his lantern and picked up the calf. It was wet and slippery, all legs. "Don't drop her!" Jenna yelled above the roar of the water. She picked up the two lanterns and led the way back to the pickup. Tim followed along in his big boots, hanging onto the squirming calf, as lightning flashed around them.

Teddy came from behind the truck. He'd found the other calf in the water, but it was too late. He gently laid it on the tailgate and shook his head.

Tim was about to lay the other calf there too, when Jenna took it from him and put it on the front seat next to Teddy. She went around and got into the back of the pickup. She motioned for Tim to get in beside her. She sat cross-legged with her back to Tim, as they bounced along in the rain, back to the cattle shed. Teddy carried the baby by his side, into a stall filled with fresh hay.

Jenna disappeared, then came back with towels and a bottle of milk with a nipple on top. "Here, you dry her off while I feed her," Jenna said as she flung the towels at Tim. The little black calf was shivering and trembling all over. Tim rubbed her dry and looked into those big, brown eyes that seemed to be saying "thanks." Half the bottle was gone and she was starting to settle down.

"It's a good sign she's takin' nourishment. Her mama's on the other side a the creek. Who knows when I'll get to 'er," Teddy stated.

"Teddy, this is Tim McConnell, Jake's great nephew. The one I was telling you about. This is Theodore Johnson. We call him 'Teddy'. That's exactly what he is too, a cuddly teddy bear." Jenna placed her arm around the old man's shoulder. "Teddy's worked here as long as I can remember."

He held his hand out to Tim. "Thanks for helpin' with the calf. We coulda' lost 'em both." The two men shook hands.

Tim liked him immediately. "No problem," was all Tim could manage to say.

The storm raged on outside the shed and the timbers creaked in the rafters above their heads. It was well past eleven when Tim and Jenna finally walked back to the house. Jenna was still in her rain bonnet and Tim in his "Isaac Walton" outfit. In the dim light of the kitchen, they looked at each other like two drowned rats and suddenly broke out laughing.

From her bedroom next to the kitchen, Annie thought how good it was to hear laughter in the house again.

Chapter 2

He was still dressed, when a sound awakened him the next morning. Sunlight sliced through a crack in the yellowed, old window shade. He sat up suddenly, knowing that it must be getting late. It was so quiet. Maybe Jake and Annie didn't get up very early. When Jenna had said goodnight, she mentioned she'd see him at breakfast. Tim put up the crisp paper shade and sunlight spread across the room. He looked at his watch—nine o'clock! *Damn, how could I have slept so late? I wanted to get an early start and I haven't even had a chance to talk to Jake and Annie about moving to town.* He wasn't even sure how to approach the subject.

His luggage was still in the car, so he straightened his rumpled clothes and put on his shoes. In the corner of his room was a pitcher of water and a bowl. There were no towels, but Tim washed his face and could feel his overnight beard itch as he looked into the mirror. The sight was frightening. His expensive haircut was usually perfect, but this morning his hair looked like a haystack and his eyes were red and droopy. *Is this what one day in the country can do?*

His room was full of antiques and dust. He could see its haze as the light filtered through the window. Spider webs made intricate patterns in every corner. Tim went down the wide old curved staircase lined with portraits of people. *Probably my ancestors,* he thought.

He went into the kitchen where dirty dishes covered the table from breakfast, but no one was around. Tim found Jake, Annie and Jenna in the cattle shed, watching Teddy feed the new calf. They turned around looking at him like proud new parents at a christening. He had to admit, the little calf was kind of cute.

"Good morning, Timothy," smiled Jake. "Sorry you missed breakfast, but we knew you were tired, so we let you sleep."

Tim nodded to everyone, "I'm going to get my luggage and clean up a bit." After he shaved and took a bath in the old claw foot tub down the hall, he dressed in jeans, sweatshirt and boots. Maybe he wouldn't look so completely out of place today.

Jake and Annie were at the kitchen table having coffee and Jenna was nowhere to be seen. "She has to go to work at noon at the little country store just down the road," Jake explained. This might be Tim's chance to say something, but where should he begin? Although it was a fairly new concept for him, he decided that honesty was the best policy.

"Uncle Jake, Annie, I don't know how to begin this conversation except to say that I'm here to help you in any way that I can. I know this has always been your home and I understand that after eighty years, change must seem very scary. But, Dr. Davis says that your health needs much more attention than it's been getting out here. He feels you'd both be better off in town, near medical help. He's worried about you. I'm your family and I want to help you make this move as comfortable as possible."

"Timothy, we know exactly why you're here. We're pleased that you have come to visit, but we're just fine here. Jenna checks in on us everyday. Teddy lives above the carriage house and we're perfectly capable of taking care of each other," Jake said decidedly.

They all sat there in silence for a few moments. Suddenly, Jake blurted out, "The family money is gone. Most of the land has been sold off to pay losses on the cattle." There was complete silence. Tim was stunned. "The cattle market was brutal. In one year alone we lost nearly $100 per head. With 2,000 head of cattle, ready for market, that was a $200,000 loss, all in one shot." Annie squirmed in her chair as Jake went on, "The railroad went broke. The tracks have been torn up and removed. The lumber business went bankrupt and the mill has been sold to a local company. California wineries took over most of our wine business. There are a few local vineyards still going, ours isn't. The last 200 acres and the buildings are mortgaged at the bank for $150,000." Jake took a deep breath and was glad it was finally out in the open.

Tim felt ill. There had been virtually no income off this place for more than ten years. The losses were only covered by selling off the assets. Years of bad management had eaten up everything. He realized that though Jake was a good person who loved this place with all his heart, he had no head for business and had probably never done a physical day's work in his life. He'd lived off his inheritance and never gave anything back. Between mismanagement and hard times in agriculture, the family fortune had dwindled to his house and the little area around it.

The taxes alone were more than the few cattle could possibly make on a good year. Tim could see why the place was in such shambles. There was simply no money for repairs. He wondered how they even paid for groceries and electricity.

Jake and Annie both cried from time to time during the conversations. They had been a proud couple, admired and respected in their younger days, by a community that now looked on them with pity. "We don't want charity. We've always been the ones to give, not to receive. I didn't want to ask the family for help either. I've let everyone down by losing so much of our inheritance."

Tim was touched by the old couple's sad story. He left the kitchen saying only, "We'll work this out. Somehow, we'll work this out. Don't worry."

He went directly out to his car and drove towards town. He went past the little store where Jenna worked. He'd stop on the way back. He needed time to think. On one hand, he felt sorry for Jake and Annie; but, on the other hand, he was angry that they let everything slip away that his ancestors spent a lifetime building.

Tim drove to Blakesburg about ten miles away. He stopped near town and used his cell phone to call his father in Chicago. After a lengthy discussion of the situation, they agreed that Tim would stay and find out as much as possible locally, while his father would find out the legalities from the family lawyer. They agreed to talk again in a day or two to compare notes.

Tim's first stop was at Dr. Davis's office. The waiting room was full of patients and Tim didn't relish the idea of waiting, but he gave his name to the receptionist and sat down.

Three small children with runny noses sat on the floor surrounded by blocks and toy trucks. One small boy cried the entire time. A cute little two-year old took the pacifier from her mouth and handed it to Tim, slobber and all. He tried to smile as he stuck it back in her mouth and wiped his hand on his jeans. *More germs per square inch than anywhere else on earth,* Tim thought to himself.

It was only a short time until the nurse called his name and led him to the doctor's private office. Tim sat there for awhile reading the diplomas on the wall. He sat in the black leather chair in front of the files stacked on a large oak desk.

Dr. Davis must be a very busy man, he thought.

Blakesburg was a thriving little town of about 20,000 people. It had this nice clinic and a small hospital. A new set of golf clubs sat in the corner and Tim recognized the paintings on the wall. Yes, Dr. Davis was doing okay.

Tim picked up the large pewter frame on the desk and turned it around. *Well, well, a picture of Jenna Adams riding a black horse. So there is something going on between Jenna and the doctor.* Jenna was dark and truly beautiful in the photo. In fact, she was gorgeous. Tim hadn't taken much notice of her appearance the night before. They started off on the wrong foot and as the stormy night wore on, he really hadn't taken a good look at her. He certainly hadn't been attracted to her. *Maybe it was that goofy-looking rain bonnet,* Tim thought with a smile. He set the picture back on the desk as the doctor walked in.

"Hello, Mr. McConnell. I'm Charles Davis"

"Nice to meet you, doctor. I don't want to take up too much of your time, but I'd like to talk to you about my aunt and uncle," Tim said as they shook hands.

Dr. Davis knew about the financial problems and told Tim that if all else failed, the couple could go into a nursing home by turning over everything to the state and going on welfare. "The nursing home would take their Social Security check each month and the state would pay the balance," he said. "I wrote your family, because their health had worsened over the winter and I thought it wasn't the neighbor's obligation to take care of them anymore."

"Do you mean Jenna Adams?"

"Well, Jenna does spend most of her spare time there. She's young and needs a life of her own. She has looked after them since she was a kid. I think it's someone else's turn, don't you?"

Tim agreed that the family hadn't done their duty, but nobody realized the state of things here, until now. He thanked the doctor for his concern and said he'd speak to him again when something was decided.

His next stop was the bank. He explained who he was and was introduced to the loan officer in charge of the mortgage. Richard Mendelson was a jerk, a vice-president of the bank who took his job way too seriously. Mr. Mendelson could hardly wait for the elder McConnells to get out of the house so it could be sold or paid-off. "I need $10,000 by the end of next month or we'll start foreclosure proceedings." To say that Tim disliked Mr. Mendelson would be an understatement. However, he could also see the bank's position; after all business is business. As Tim left, he realized that some decisions would have to be made soon.

He drove around town. Blakesburg was an old river town with old money. There was a private college with a beautiful campus, a new industrial park, several golf courses and a huge office complex with a large adjoining shopping mall. Beautiful new homes dotted the outskirts of town, while old Victorian homes looked over the bluffs along the river.

He stopped and inquired about rates at two nursing homes and a retirement village. Nothing was less than $2,000 a month. That would be $4,000 for two people. Jake and Annebelle definitely would need help, but were they ill enough to go to a nursing home? There had to be a better solution.

Tim went into a couple of real estate offices. He explained that he was a realtor from Chicago. No one seemed impressed. One lady gave him a few suggestions, but seemed skeptical about really helping him. "There are some low income housing units available. Maybe a nurse could come in a few times a week to help." He'd have to talk that over with Jake and his father. He left town feeling depressed and discouraged. All he could do now was go back to the house and see what was left to sell.

* * *

As he came to the intersection by the country store, Tim noticed Jenna getting into her car. It was 5:15; she was getting off work. He pulled up beside her and got out.

"Hi," he said awkwardly.

"Hello. Are you coming from town?"

"Yes, I went to see your favorite doctor."

"He's not *my* doctor!" she snapped back.

"Sorry, I noticed your picture on his desk, and I just assumed you were close."

"We are friends, but don't assume too much."

"Listen, Jenna. Let's start over. Do you have time to talk?"

She got out of her car. "Let's go inside and have some coffee," she said reluctantly, as she unlocked the door and turned on the lights.

It smelled wonderful inside the little store. Tim had no idea where the aroma was coming from, but it filled the air with cinnamon and spices. The old wood flooring, the potbellied stove, old scales and antique counter took him back to another place in time. There was a glass candy counter filled with old-fashioned stick candy and jawbreakers. Barrels of coffee beans and shelves filled with foods lined the walls. The ceiling was covered with hanging baskets filled with dried florals and herbs. Around the old stove were tables and chairs, where Jenna explained, "The men in the neighborhood meet here mornings for coffee and donuts. They gossip and pull practical jokes. Afternoons, the ladies come in to take over the gossip. I find out everything that's going on around here. We have some real characters stop by."

Martin's Mercantile had been there for over 100 years, owned by different people under different names, but always a comfortable and cozy place to gather and swap tales. Jenna loved working there for Sarah Martin. Sarah had hired her as a teenager and had been a wonderful friend and advisor ever since Jenna's parents died in a car crash 15 years ago. "I could have made a lot more money working in Blakesburg, but I owe Sarah and I love my job. I live in an apartment above Sarah's garage, just down the road. It's small, but all I really need."

Jenna brought coffee and some cookies to the table and motioned for Tim to join her. They sat down and slowly started talking, first about the store, then about Jenna's childhood. They talked for hours. Tim drank his coffee and watched her. She was at home here, not so threatened by him, not so defensive. She told him how the McConnells had helped her grandparents save their farm during the depression. "Not only my family, but lots of families in the area received help over the years, in one way or another, from Jake and Annie."

"At Christmas, Jake saw to it that the kids in the area had toys and candy, even when times were bad. Presents were left outside on Christmas Eve, signed 'Love, Santa'. Grocery and doctor bills were paid when money was short. Everyone knew it was Jake, but no one ever spoke of it."

The little country community hated the situation that Jake and Annie were in now, even though some of it was their own fault. "The only help they will accept is my stopping to look in on them from time to time. I've always been close to them." She was probably Annie's only real friend. "In the glory days, Annie was a bit of an outsider. She was too wealthy, and didn't seem to fit into the rural culture. Now, she is just quiet and lonely."

Jenna had played at the big house, even when she was small. Jake and Annie adored her. "They lost their only child at age 3 and took me into their hearts as if I was their own." Annie would let Jenna dress up in the old clothes around the house and they'd pretend to have tea on the verandah. "Annie taught me to make dolls from hollyhocks growing along the roadside ditch, and how to brush my hair 100 strokes each night." They were soul mates. "After my parents died, I moved in with Jake and Annie for awhile." She was 18 years old and very alone. They loved her and grieved with her until she could stand on her own.

"Sarah Martin and her husband made the attic above their garage into an apartment and encouraged me to move in and start a new life. I've been there ever since."

Tim interrupted only to ask, "Isn't it a little lonely out here so far from town?"

She told him that Sarah was constantly playing matchmaker. "Most of my friends from high school moved on to college or marriage a long time ago." She'd dated some, but nothing serious. "Then I met Dr. Davis during a visit to his office with Jake and

Annie. We've been going out ever since. No one ever swept me off my feet before. Chuck took me dining and dancing, we played golf and tennis at the country club and I was hostess at his cocktail parties in his home that overlooks the river. After a trip to the Bahamas, he asked me to move in with him. I did, but within a few months, I felt trapped."

He had given her everything; clothes, money, prestige. Everything a young woman from the country could ever dream of. He was fun to be with, but she didn't love him. "He wanted all my time and energy. He wanted me to quit my job and he's jealous of the time I spend with Jake and Annie. He was always at the office or the hospital, but wanted me to be home, just in case he might show up. He thought of me as a possession, not a person. I left him almost six months ago and moved back to Sarah's apartment. We still see each other occasionally."

Jenna couldn't believe that she was telling all of this to a total stranger. At first she had just wanted Tim to understand how she felt about Jake and Annie. The more she talked the more personal the conversation had become. Tim had really listened to her, something the doctor had never done. They sat there in the dim light of the little store, as Jenna rattled on and on.

She told him all about Jake and Annie and how much they loved the old way of life, when times were good. "Jake is living in the past now, I'm worried about him. I wonder what might happen if he was forced to move out of the house. Annie keeps everything just as it was when she married him, 60 years ago. He wants it that way, he knows immediately if anything has been moved. He scolds her for moving his precious belongings and tells her that his beautiful mother would be displeased. The past and the present are all meshed as one, and Jake can't always tell one from the other."

Tim told Jenna about the long talk he had with them earlier that day and how he now understood about their finances. She couldn't believe how candid they were with him about such delicate matters. They rarely spoke about their money to anyone. But why was she so surprised, she had just told her life story to a guy she didn't know until yesterday at this time. Tim had a way of getting people to tell him things they weren't used to sharing. That's how he made a living in real estate. People often gave him more information than they meant to and Tim had a reputation for using it against them later.

They discussed the bank's threat of foreclosure and how much it would cost to move Jake and Annie to town, which Jenna wanted no part of. They went over the possibilities several times, and then decided to sleep on the information and make some decisions the next day. They said goodnight outside the store and went their separate ways. They each had a lot to think about.

Chapter 3

The next morning Tim was up at dawn. He had arrived back at the house late the night before. Jake and Annie were already in bed and Tim was glad. It had been a very emotional day and he had tossed and turned all night. He wasn't used to taking on other people's problems. But, for some reason, the events of the day had upset him. When he finally fell asleep, he dreamed of the old house with Jake dressing up as Santa Claus and Annie crying over her lost baby. Tim awoke more exhausted than when he went to bed.

He dressed quietly and went outside. He wandered around the grounds, actually looking at the place for the first time. The air smelled fresh and clean. The birds were chirping and singing. All around him, little crocuses were popping out of the ground. The trees were budding and out across the woods, little pink and white blossoms dotted the landscape. The dogwoods were all in bloom. It was God's way of showing that spring had arrived, a time for hope and renewal.

The sun felt good on his face as he walked out to the cattle shed. The little calf lay next to its mama and they looked content there in the early morning light. Teddy came across the drive from the carriage house and handed Tim a cup of coffee. "I saw ya' come down from outta the house," he said. "Up kinda early ain't ya'?"

"Couldn't sleep."

They sat down on a bale of straw and drank the strong black coffee. Steam rose from the cups in the cool morning air. "Best time a' day."

"Yep," Tim agreed, though he'd seldom seen a sunrise.

It was peaceful and calming to sit there watching the sky change from lavender to bright blue in the sunlight. The rain had washed everything clean and Tim just wanted to breathe in the cool, wonderful fresh air.

The old shaggy dog wandered in to lie down at Teddy's feet. His name was Gus. "Jenna named him after the mailman when she was six. She'd talk about Gus and nobody knew whether she meant the mailman or the dog, so we call him 'Gus the dog'". Gus was nearly ninety in dog years. He was blind in one eye and suffered from arthritis. But, like everything else on the place, he was left in the same routine day after day as in years gone by. No one had the heart to put him to sleep.

Teddy and Gus gave Tim the tour of the buildings. Gus lay down every chance he had. Teddy explained that the unique round brick barn had once been used for showing and judging cattle. It sat empty now, with seats for nearly 200 people. There were only two others like it in the state. The white trim and doors needed paint just like the house. Tim's real estate mind was trying to put a price on it. *What would anyone use it for way out here in the middle of nowhere?*

The old carriage house was brick, also. Inside were old buggies and wagons that smelled of musty leather; some in pieces, some missing wheels. Dusty tack hung from every wall. The brass trim was tarnished and dull. Tim had no idea how much old horse harnesses and wagons were worth.

Teddy explained that he lived upstairs in the loft. He was in his mid-70's now and had trouble getting up the steep stairs at night. "I'm not complainin' though. I love this place. It's my home." He spoke of Jake and Annie with much affection. They'd been good to him through the years. He had no formal education, but Annie had taught him his letters and numbers at the kitchen table years ago.

"They never talk down to me just 'cuz I was the hired help. They treat me with respect. I'm gettin' old now and can't do much for 'em anymore. But they need me and I do what I can." A tear came to his eye as he told Tim of the time Annie nursed him back to health, after a deadly flu epidemic. Several of the neighbors died that winter, but Annie brought him soup each day and bathed his head with cool water until his fever broke. He owed her his life. "She's a good woman."

They walked out along the dilapidated old fences that lined the drive. "This was a showplace ya' know. I feel bad I couldn't keep it that way."

"I know," Tim said as he patted Teddy on the back, "I know."

They walked back towards the house. Gus the dog had given out on them and lay down in the middle of the drive to rest. Behind the house at the edge of the woods was a guest cottage. The old brick path was overgrown with weeds and brush, but Teddy led the way like a guide on safari. It was a small house, built of native stone; the servant quarters at one time. There was a big stone fireplace right up through the middle. It was basically one large room, with some of the windows broken and only a bird's nest seen in the beams above. Teddy suddenly became very quiet and they moved on quickly without another word.

There were old trails through the underbrush out to the pastures and on to Willow Creek. The creek looked placid and lazy on this beautiful spring morning, not at all like the raging river it had become just two days before in the flood. The water was back in its banks. *What a difference a day makes*, Tim thought to himself.

The tour ended abruptly. Teddy just disappeared without saying a word. Tim found his way back to the house. Inside, the kitchen smelled of bacon and eggs. Annie nodded and Jake shoved a chair toward him. They were particularly quiet this morning. Tim decided they weren't sure what to say. He started the conversation with, "I went to Blakesburg yesterday." Silence. "I visited with Dr. Davis and Mr. Mendelson at the bank." No response.

"Did I ever tell you about the time my father owned most of the shares in that bank?" Jake tried to change the subject. "It was during the Depression. The bank closed, just like so many of them did that year. My father bought the bank and opened it three days later. It was the only one around for awhile. Kept things going around here when other people were jumping out of four-story buildings in St. Louis." He was off again in days gone by. Tim suspected it was his way of coping; denial.

Tim called his father later that day. James had spoken with the lawyer and learned that Jake had the legal say on the estate. Unless he was proven mentally incompetent, Jake had to give his approval on any legal transactions. Tim's hands would be tied as far as selling the property was concerned, unless Jake agreed to it. That seemed unlikely. Tim explained how things stood at the bank and how expensive it would be to put Jake and Annie in a home. Tim's father had called an appraiser in Kansas City who knew antiques and would be at the estate in the morning to decide just how much everything was worth. Tim wasn't sure how much they could get for the house and land, but it probably wouldn't cover the mortgage at the bank. The two decided to talk again in a few days.

Tim called Jenna at work that afternoon and told her about the appraiser. "He's coming tomorrow morning at 10:00." Tim could tell she was not happy about the idea. Later she arrived at the house with a man in a suit. They marched right past Tim in the hall, went into the kitchen with Jake and Annie and slammed the door. Tim couldn't hear the conversation, but Jenna was doing most of the talking.

They came out of the kitchen about twenty minutes later. Jenna announced, "I now have Power of Attorney for Jake and Annie, and I will act in their best interest." She was angry again. It was as if their long conversation the night before had never happened.

"I told you it would be over my dead body that you take them from this place. I told you that the very first day that you were here. Haven't you heard a word we've told you?" she asked as she stormed out with her attorney.

The appraiser arrived at 10:00 the next morning as promised. Robert Ellis was a tall thin, serious man in a three-piece suit. Jenna arrived a few minutes later. She didn't say a word, but shook hands with Mr. Ellis when Tim introduced them. Jake led the way through the old house, answering the appraiser's questions regarding the age of the different pieces of furniture and dishes. He gave lots of information and history on each piece.

Tim knew nothing about antiques. He had decided long ago that it was just old junk. He had no interest in owning any of it, but as they wandered through the house, he couldn't help becoming more intrigued by its history.

Lots of pieces were one of a kind and, other than being dirty, were in perfect condition. "The black lacquered oriental chests were brought home from the Emperor of China. The pieces carved of solid ivory are from India," Jake explained. Brass and crystal, pewter and silver were all tarnished and dull but unique and beautiful at one time. There was a set of dishes from the World's Fair, the only set in existence. "There are twenty-four place settings, all trimmed in gold." Large silver coffee services and chafing dishes, once bright, were now black with tarnish. The long Queen Anne mahogany table and chair set was beautifully detailed to seat 16 easily, 18 if needed.

Upstairs there were brass beds, oriental rugs, tapestries, portraits, old toys and dollhouses, quilts and down comforters; all shrouded in dust and cobwebs. The old bare light bulb in each room didn't allow enough light to truly see the wonderful treasurers.

One room was filled with music boxes, some revolving, some not. A tiny porcelain baby in a rocking cradle brought tears to Jake's eyes. He held and caressed each item as he spoke about it. These were his children; his joy, his whole existence. There wasn't a single piece in the whole house that Jake didn't love and cherish.

The appraiser took inventory and notes on each piece. He looked at many items with a magnifying glass. Other things he scratched with a fingernail or sniffed and thumped with his finger.

The library was full of old, dusty books. Jake enjoyed telling about one in particular, it was an old road atlas of sorts. It was printed before any main roads existed and gave directions to get from St. Louis to Kansas City. It read, "Go to the large oak tree near Clayton Ridge, take the left fork to the hickory grove near Tilton Creek, at the bottom of the hill, turn left," and on and on. Even Jenna laughed at that. Jake remarked, "The hardest part was trying to get back to St. Louis. It was much harder to read the directions backward."

They took a break at noon for a sandwich. Annebelle stayed in the kitchen. The antiques were Jake's treasures, not hers. The appraiser wrote more notes and didn't speak except to ask questions about an origin or age. He went back to the library and spent another hour and a half cataloging books. Tim, Jake and Jenna sat silently as the appraiser looked through hat boxes filled with Valentines and old letters. They didn't quite know what to say to each other.

There were wonderful porcelain vases and a collection of tiny china dolls, untouched, except by age. The third floor was stacked with trunks full of clothing and linens, extra furniture, toys, pictures and more books. The cellar held cobwebbed treasures of days gone by; old crocks, blue glass jars, lanterns, old decoys and fishing equipment.

The summer kitchen housed a huge old cook stove, copper boilers, baskets of every size and shape, an old dry sink, butter churns, washboards, tubs and an old wringer-style washer. Clotheslines criss-crossed the ceiling, like old shoe laces.

It was well after five o'clock when Tim and Jenna took the appraiser out to the carriage house. It was late when he left. "I'll send a written report within a week, along with the bill," the appraiser said, as he shook hands with Tim and headed for his car.

"I'm not very happy that you and your father took it upon yourselves to find an appraiser. Don't you think Jake should have made that decision," Jenna asked as she and Tim walked towards the kitchen. "You're very pushy, Tim McConnell."

Everyone was tired. After an uncomfortably quiet supper, Tim said his "goodnights" and went up to bed. Somehow he had become the enemy again, and he didn't like being put in that awkward position. *Hopefully the money will make it all worthwhile*, Tim thought. *It usually does.*

Chapter 4

Waiting for the appraisal was a nail-biting experience for Tim. No one was talking to him unless they had to. The appraiser had called several times, speaking only to Jake, asking more questions about the age or origin of different pieces, never giving a clue as to his opinion. Tim was getting antsy. The cold shoulder he was receiving from Jake made mealtimes painful, so Tim avoided the house as much as possible. He got into his car each morning and wandered the countryside most of the day. He tried to call Ellen but always got the answering machine. Evenings were long and lonely and Tim found himself at a small roadhouse just outside of Blakesburg, almost every night. At least there, no one was angry at him.

He sat at the bar having a beer. The bartender was drying glasses and telling Tim about bass fishing. Two young men, who apparently lived nearby, were playing pool for money and were taking the game very seriously. Tim's mind wandered from the bartender's bass story to this morning's sparing match with Jenna. He had stopped at the little country store for a cup of coffee and a donut, but she wouldn't leave him alone. She loudly introduced him to the local cronies, "This is the big wheel from Chicago who is here trying to take Jake and Annie from their beloved home."

Tim was mortified. He got up and went outside, his face red from embarrassment. He wasn't used to this kind of treatment. He should have said something or marched right back in and explained that he was just trying to help. But, as he turned around, he saw faces watching him from the window and all he could do was get into the car and leave.

He was trying to help, wasn't he? Maybe Jenna was right, maybe he was here looking out only for himself. He drove around all morning thinking about his real motives for being there. Tim had a reputation for being cold and manipulative with people. Real estate was a dog-eat-dog business in the 90's, especially in Chicago. Sentimentality had no place in Tim's world. He had never really done anything illegal, but unethical was a different story. So he undercut a price. So the plumbing wasn't up to code. No big deal, business is business. "People get what they deserve," had been Tim's motto.

His parents had seen this hard side of him grow gradually over the past few years. They had hoped he'd find a girl who would soften his heart, but he just seemed more distant and angry with each new relationship and every new business deal. Ellen certainly wasn't their choice for Tim. Her insecurity and resentment of their wealth only made Tim more focused on making his own money, no matter how he had to do it. She seemed to make Tim feel guilty for being born with money. Now he was constantly on a mission to prove to the world that he deserved to have anything he wanted. He'd been working nearly non-stop for months, always at a meeting or on the phone. His parents had to make an appointment just to talk to him. They had hoped this trip to the old homestead would get him away from the stress of the city for awhile and away from Ellen.

James could hear the frustration in Tim's voice every time he called. Was it somehow their fault that Tim was so money hungry and angry? He had never wanted for anything as a child. They had spoiled him. They were busy with their careers and felt guilty about not spending time with him. They gave Tim anything he wanted: toys, clothes, cars, private schools, trips. Now they were paying the ultimate price. They had to watch the son they loved, become an unscrupulous businessman, successful but not respected.

Respect was important to the old McConnell name. Tim's grandfather, Jonathan McConnell III, was old Jake's brother. Jonathan and Jake had been inseparable as children. They traveled the world with their parents and learned the good life at an early age. Jake had stayed home to learn the cattle business while Jonathan went off to college in Chicago, where he became a very successful stock broker after the crash of '29. He married Tim's grandmother and had only one child, James, Tim's father. Their family became an important part of Chicago society. As the years went by, they went back to the homestead less and less. By the time Jake and Jonathan's parents died, the two brothers had become virtual strangers.

Jake was awarded the homestead and local holdings, while Jonathan inherited the stocks, bonds and foreign investments acquired over the years. Everything Jonathan touched turned to gold, while Jake, with no head for business, lost nearly everything around him. His father never took the time to teach Jake the cattle business or anything else for that matter. There was always enough money, so he really never had to work.

Jake was ashamed and never let Jonathan know of his misfortunes. The two slowly drifted apart. Jonathan remembered his childhood home with affection and his parents with respect. The family name meant everything to him and he told his son and later his grandson, Tim, all about the old family home and fortune. He died believing it all remained intact.

After his grandfather died, Tim's parents, James and Lisa, never kept in touch with Jake and Annie. They assumed that the elderly couple were rich and comfortable in their old age. They assumed wrong. They would be shocked now, to see the way Jake and Annie were living, basically existing in their room next to the kitchen with only a small fireplace to keep them warm and only a few dimly lit bulbs in that huge house. They barely had enough to eat.

An attractive young girl sat down on the barstool next to Tim and ordered a drink. Just then, a noisy group of couples came bouncing through the door. Tim and the girl next to him turned in unison to see them. It was Jenna, Dr. Davis and some friends. *What a wonderful smile she has*, Tim thought. It was the first time he'd seen it since late that first stormy night. It seemed to light up the entire room. She wore a little red dress and heels. Tim had never seen her in anything but jeans. She was gorgeous. *Why doesn't she smile more often*, he wondered? She always seemed to be angry, but tonight she was having fun.

The doctor came over to order drinks and said "hello" to Tim. Tim nodded in reply and slid closer to the girl next to him to make room for the doctor's friends. Jenna and the ladies in the group went to sit down at a large round table in the corner. As she pulled out a chair, she noticed Tim at the bar. Their eyes met for a moment. She noticed him sitting very close to a lovely young girl and Jenna's wonderful smile suddenly disappeared.

Chapter 5

Early Monday morning, a courier van drove up the driveway. Tim and Jake both went to the door. Jake signed for the large manila envelope in the driver's hand. They took it back to the kitchen table, where trembling, Jake slowly opened it. Annie sat quietly at the table with a cup of tea, while Tim waited for the results with anticipation. Inside was a ream of paper with computer printouts listing furniture, dishes, books, even the old tack from the carriage house.

Jake handed Tim the cover letter and asked him to read it aloud:

Dear Mr. McConnell:

It was my great honor to meet you and come into your home to place a monetary value on your treasured belongings. My associates and I have come up with what we feel would be a conservative estimate of their value. Taking into consideration the fact that you have several one-of-a-kind items, we feel that some of those items may be considered by many to be priceless. We have marked them accordingly in our report. You may want to contact the Historical Society or various museums to sell those particular items.

As for the majority of this collection, my colleagues and I would consider it our privilege to help you arrange for an auction. We have an auction house in mind, in St. Louis, that might be large enough to handle a transaction of this magnitude.

Please contact us at your convenience if we can be of further help.

Respectfully, Robert D. Ellis

Attached was the bill and appraisal fee for $17,500. Tim nearly had a stroke. He hurriedly flipped through the pages of the appraisal and there at the very bottom was Mr. Ellis' "conservative" estimate of $3.5 million dollars. The fee was only ½ of 1%.

Tim spent the rest of the morning trying to explain to Jake and Annie exactly what this wonderful news meant. "Finally, you can enjoy life again. You can sell the land and homestead, auction off your belongings and invest the money. You can reap the rewards, move to Blakesburg, or Florida or Hawaii and be taken care of for the rest of your lives."

Jake was confused and a bit overwhelmed. "I don't want to sell anything. Maybe now the bank can lend me money to live on. They can use the antiques as collateral.

Tim argued, "There will be no way to pay a loan back, unless you sell the antiques. Maybe you could keep some of your favorite belongings, but the rest will have to go. Anyway, your health needs attention and that will cost a lot, no matter where you go."

The two men argued, put down figures on paper, then argued some more. It went on most of the morning when finally, Jake announced, "I'm going to call Jenna. She'll know what to do." He got up and went to the phone.

Tim looked across the table at little Annie. She looked bewildered and sad. He reached across the table and touched her hand. Her tired eyes looked right through him as she rose from the table and went out to the verandah. Annie closed the door behind her and gazed off into the distance. The sun had warmed the early April morning and she looked longingly toward the little graveyard on the hill across the road. It was there, in the clearing in the woods, where she and Jake buried their tiny baby girl, Marisa, so many years ago. She'd visited her little one often and taken fresh flowers to lay lovingly beside the small stone statue of a lamb. *The Lamb of God*, Annie thought to herself. Her heart had broken when Marisa died and the pieces were too scattered now to ever be whole again.

Annie had always felt like an outsider here. The McConnell family never really embraced her. The community only half-heartedly accepted her and only because she was married to Jake. She'd never been truly happy, but she could never leave. Her baby was here and so was her husband. He loved her in his own way. Besides, it wasn't his fault that nothing could fill this huge void in her soul.

It wasn't long until Jenna drove into the drive and hurried up to the house. She knowingly wrapped her arms around Annie and helped her back inside, where Tim and Jake's conversation had come to a standstill. Jake was stubborn and uncompromising, while Tim seemed overbearing and a real know-it-all. They were getting nowhere.

Jenna sat down to mediate and with Annie by her side, they started over. Tim brought Jenna up to speed with the appraisal. She was shocked by the values, "Even the dusty old family photos are worth thousands of dollars," Tim pointed out.

She understood Jake's reluctance to sell anything, but she knew Tim was right. "Some things will have to be sold in order to preserve the rest," she explained to Jake. "I know it will be painful, but you will have to make some choices."

By late afternoon the negotiations had come to an end, at least for the day. Tim had compromised by agreeing that Jake and Annie could stay in the house with the help of a part-time nurse. "But, you'll have to sell off enough to fix up the house, pay off the bank and have enough money to eat properly and take care of yourselves." This was a big step for both Tim and Jake. They stood up and shook hands on it. Tim hugged Annie and was glad the tension between them was finally over. He started to hug Jenna, then after an awkward moment, they shook hands instead. They all sighed a collective sigh of relief and then laughed out loud.

Tim offered to take them all out to dinner to celebrate, but Jake and Annie declined. They were exhausted by the days' events. Tim looked over at Jenna, "How about you, Miss Adams?"

She couldn't think of an excuse fast enough and before she could say anything, he had grabbed her arm. "Let's go somewhere nice.

It's my treat. I'll pick you up in an hour." Jenna said a quick good-bye to Jake and Annie and flashed that radiant smile at Tim.

An hour later, they sat side by side in Tim's car, winding down the road toward Blakesburg. He had picked her up right on time. He was looking forward to not eating alone. *A little human companionship will be wonderful*, he thought.

I'm so nervous, but why? This isn't like a real date or anything, just dinner. I've taken hundreds of women out for dinner. Well, not hundreds, but a lot. After all, she is involved with the doctor and I have Ellen. (He made a mental note to call Ellen tomorrow. He hadn't talked to her for several days. She kept leaving messages, but he hadn't called her back. They seemed to be playing phone tag.)

Jenna sat quietly beside him. She was impressed. He had come to the door looking like someone out of GQ magazine. He wore a black T-shirt and slacks with a gray sport coat. She liked what she saw. Her heart skipped a beat and she was embarrassed by her own feelings. She had felt a little jealous the week before when she saw him at the roadhouse sitting next to that pretty young girl. *How stupid! Jealous about what? All we ever do is argue, but not today.* "Today you were wonderful!" *Did I say that out loud?*

"Wonderful about what?"

I did say it out loud. Oh, Lord! "Well, about Jake, you know," she said hurriedly.

"No, you were wonderful. You made Jake see my side and I hate to admit it, but you made me understand him a little, too. We weren't getting anywhere until you came in."

46

"Well, you are both very stubborn. It must run in the family."

They pulled up at a little Italian restaurant that hung out over the cliffs above the river. The sun had already set, but a soft purple glow still hung in the sky. Tim opened her door and couldn't help but notice her gorgeous legs as they swung out to stand near him. *She looks beautiful tonight. More relaxed, less defensive, and oh, those eyes!*

They ordered a bottle of wine and looked out the window toward the river. The lights from the restaurant danced across the water. They didn't talk, but she could feel him looking at her from across the table.

What is going on here? Are we attracted to each other? Jenna hadn't felt this way for a very long time. That funny little feeling in the pit of her stomach. *Oh, snap out of it,* she thought. *You're just hungry.*

"I don't know what to say to you." Jenna said, just to break the silence.

"We don't have to say anything, do we?"

"No, I just get nervous when things are too quiet. It seems like all we've done is argue since you got here."

Tim smiled, "Well, let's stop that. We don't have to talk about Jake or Annie or the house or anything else that might set you off."

"Set me off!" Jenna snapped. "There are always two sides to an argument," she stated as she raised her hand in the air.

"I'm sorry. I set you off again, didn't I?" Tim grinned a sweet, impish grin and grabbed the hand she seemed most likely to strike him with. He gently squeezed it and brought it back down to the table, before she could tip over her wine glass. He left his hand over hers and said, "Jenna, I know I upset you, but I'm not your enemy. I'm trying to understand this whole situation, too. I know you are looking out for Jake and Annie, but give me a chance, I'm not here to hurt them."

Jenna pulled her hand away, "I know that, but you don't know them or me, for that matter. You don't know how important that old house is to us."

"Then help me to understand. I'd like to know you Jenna, not as Jake's protector, but as Jenna Adams. Jenna Adams, the beautiful woman with a good heart and a passion for life. Not the angry, fearful Jenna, who strikes out when anyone gets too close."

Jenna calmed down and took a deep breath. "I'm sorry. I don't mean to be angry, but I can't quite figure out your true motive for being here."

Tim placed his hand over hers again, "Jenna, at this very moment, I can't figure it out either." He smiled at her and this time she returned the smile; that beautiful smile.

Their food came and with a couple more glasses of wine, the warm fuzzies set in. Their conversation became slow and easy and they finally seemed comfortable with each other. Neither of them was in a hurry to leave.

Finally, he helped her on with her coat. Her hair smelled of flowers when he brushed close to her. They walked out to the car and he waited as she swung those legs in. *Those legs again, those eyes, that smile!*

They drove home in silence, not wanting to break the wonderful spell that surrounded them. He walked her to the door and kissed her cheek. She stopped breathing and he was gone.

Chapter 6

What had seemed like a break-through the day before was fast becoming a nightmare today. Jake and Annie had started a list of things they couldn't bear to part with. The list was getting longer by the minute and Tim was growing impatient. He was trying to be understanding. *But good grief, it is just old stuff. Why wouldn't they rather have the money? Why wouldn't they rather live in comfort? They could sell the antiques and buy new things.* He didn't get it.

When Jenna arrived at ten, all that Jake had agreed to sell was the dinette set and the kitchen appliances. Tim had tried to explain that they were not even on the appraiser's list. "They aren't antiques, they're just old!" Tim was frustrated.

Jenna could see that the tension was back. She sat down and they started through the list one item at a time. By noon, they had made some progress. "We all agree that most of the items in the carriage house will have to go. We'll try to keep one carriage and one wagon, along with the appropriate harness. The sale of the rest will at least get the bank off our backs for awhile," Jenna stated.

Jenna and Tim sat side by side at the table, juggling figures with a calculator. Her hand brushed against his and he winked at her. Annie even noticed that they were getting along better today. Jenna had become the peacemaker. *I'll try to keep the two men I love from killing each other. Love? Where did that word come from,* she wondered? *I don't love Tim. I hardly know him. I mean the two men I care about. I don't want them angry with each other. After all, this arguing is hard on Annie. It's hard on everyone.*

Jenna went back to work at the store so that Jake and Annie could rest. They looked exhausted. Tim left to go see the "friendly" banker. He took the appraisal papers along. He couldn't wait to shove them in Richard Mendelson's face.

Richard was hardly impressed. "I knew all along they were hiding antiques out there," he said. "I just hope they are well-insured."

Oh, Lord. Insurance! Tim knew they couldn't have had them insured for the kind of values the appraiser had found. Tim let the remark about "hiding" antiques pass, for the time being, but he made a mental note to bring it up again, soon. The bank agreed to wait for their money until a sale could be arranged, so at least he had accomplished something.

He stopped back at the store to ask Jenna about the insurance. She phoned Jake's insurance agent who said, "The house is insured for $10,000, but Jake dropped the insurance on the contents years ago. Insurance on antiques can be very costly and every piece will have to be listed separately on the policy. To come up with the premium will be a real challenge." The situation was quickly becoming very expensive, but they had no choice but to get the insurance.

Maybe this agreement with Jake can't be worked out after all, Tim thought. *Equity just isn't going to be enough. Something has to give.*

Tim gave Jenna a peck on the cheek. He had to think. He left her there and went back to the homestead. But, he wasn't quite ready to go head to head with Jake quite yet, so he wandered down along the creek. *Why is this so hard? If only I wasn't getting so involved. Maybe the only answer is to have Jake declared incompetent, sell everything and go home,* Tim thought. *No, Jenna would be devastated.* Was he willing to lose any chance he might have with her? Something about her was driving him crazy! He closed his eyes and all he could see was her smile.

He went back to his car and called Ellen. He got her answering machine. *That stupid machine! Why isn't she ever there when I need her? She calls me a million times a day, with one stupid thing after another, but when I have a problem; she's never there. But then again, Ellen probably wouldn't think millions of dollars in antiques as a problem.*

Chapter 7

It was nearly three in the morning when the sound of Tim's cell phone by the bed woke him. It was Jenna. "Tim, can you come over? I need to see you."

"Sure, when?" he said in a stupor.

"Now! I really need you tonight. I know it's late, but, can you?"

"I'll be right over." Tim didn't know what to think. What did she mean, "she needed him?" *Is she lonely? Is she sick?* He couldn't tell by her voice. He got dressed and hurried out to the car quietly, so as not to wake Jake and Annie. He was lonely, too; more lonely than he'd ever been in his life. *If only Ellen had been home, maybe I wouldn't be out here headed for someone else. Whatever happens tonight is Ellen's fault;* he decided.

Tim got there in record time. He flew up the stairs with anticipation. Jenna was standing in a sweat suit to greet him. Her hair wasn't combed and she didn't look at all like a woman needing company. *So much for the "she's lonely" theory.* She grabbed his arm and guided him to the couch. There were papers and sketches everywhere.

"I've been up all night working on this, and I had to show you," she said excitedly.

"Couldn't it wait until tomorrow?" he asked, disgusted that she'd call for this, a bunch of figures again. The only figure he wanted to talk about tonight was hers.

"Tim, I've found the answer! It was here all the time. I know how to keep the homestead and most of the antiques and still make money. I've figured it all out. An inn, we'll make the house into a country inn, The Inn at Willow Creek! How's that sound?"

Stupid, was Tim's first reaction, but he never got a chance to say it.

"The house is a natural. We could restore it and the grounds. It's basically sound. Some elbow grease, imagination and maybe some paint could cover the years of neglect. We could make a suite from two rooms and a bath upstairs. The other bathroom could be shared by the other five bedrooms. Every bedroom has its own fireplace, too. There is plenty of furniture around. Even the appraiser said everything was in good shape, just dirty. A little dirt doesn't scare me."

"We could rent out the guest cottage for at least $200 a night. The suite, five rooms and the guest cottage, could bring in as much as $1,000 a night if every room was filled. The cost would include a full breakfast in the dining room and an afternoon tea in the solarium."

Tim wondered if she had noticed that there was no glass in the big solarium, only a few broken panes. *It's evidently only a small detail in her overall scheme of things.*

"Lunch and dinner could be served extra, lunch at $6.50 a plate and dinner at $12.00. That could bring in another $400 a day. Of course, that isn't all profit, but $1,400 a day means nearly $10,000 a week times 52 weeks. The potential for a half million gross would certainly help things along. Okay, maybe it wouldn't start out that way, but it could provide the cash flow we need to restore the house and preserve the antiques.

"Oh yes," she continued, "and the barn. We could restore it and have horse shows in it. We could rent it out for $1,000 a day; a two-day show would bring $2,000. We could have four shows a year, that's $8,000. That would be enough to repair the roof and paint the trim," she punched buttons on her calculator, figuring and refiguring.

"Dr. Thompson is a retired veterinarian. He bought some land from Jake a few years ago. It connects with the homestead, with riding trails through the woods. He boards horses over there, too. His clients are lawyers and executives from all around. Maybe they could stay at the Inn and ride their horses on the weekends. Now they stay at the hotel in Blakesburg. I'll take you over to meet Doc tomorrow." She looked at her watch, "Okay, I mean today."

"But what about the grounds?" Tim interrupted. "It looks like a jungle out there."

"I've thought about that. We can offer the students from the agricultural college in Columbia an "educational work experience". That would be a fancy name for free work, in exchange for free room and board for a month. They could get the flower gardens cleaned, the fruit trees shaped up, the grapevine trimmed, whatever needed to be done. They could stay in the house while we're fixing it up and eat with us. It could be fun."

Jenna was glowing. She seemed to have thought of everything. Everything except Jake and Annie. They were private people. What would they think of strangers staying with them, sharing their things? Well, it was an option and they didn't have many of those if they wanted to stay in the house much longer. She'd present it to them and see how they'd respond.

Jenna finally took a deep breath. She suddenly felt very tired. She offered to make breakfast, but Tim just wanted to go back to bed. They walked out to his car. This time, she kissed him. "Thanks for coming over and listening. I know I might be crazy, but it could work, couldn't it?"

He was too tired to argue, "Why not?"

One more kiss and he was gone again. The day was dawning and he could see her waving in his rearview mirror. *This early morning business is highly overrated*, he thought as he drove back to the homestead. *I need sleep!*

As he turned the corner, he could see the lights from an ambulance, flashing across the yard. Something had happened. He grabbed his cell phone and called Jenna as he pulled up into the drive. "Get over here quick! Something's wrong!"

Teddy and Jake were on the verandah and the paramedics were putting Annie into the ambulance. She had an oxygen mask on her face and her eyes were closed.

"I couldn't wake her. I couldn't make her wake up," was all Jake could say.

Tim placed his arm around Jake's old, slumped shoulders and replied, "It will be okay, Jake. I should have been here to help you."

Just then, Jenna arrived. She went directly over to the ambulance and got in. They pulled away. Tim and Jake followed in Tim's car, leaving Teddy on the verandah with tears streaming down his old, worn face.

Chapter 8

Jenna rushed down the hall when she saw Dr. Davis, "Chuck, is she going to be all right?"

"No, honey. It was a massive heart attack. It's only a matter of time. There was a lot of damage. I'm sorry." She fell into his arms and he held her close, rocking back and forth.

Seeing them together made Tim uncomfortable. He took Jake aside and tried to comfort him. "Can I see her?" Jake asked.

"I'll go find out," Tim replied.

Quietly they all slipped into her room. Annie was resting comfortably. Jenna kissed her cheek and said her good-byes. "I'll take care of Jake, I promise. I love you, Annie," she whispered close to Annie's ear.

Tim patted her tiny hand then he and Jenna went out, leaving Jake alone with his beloved wife.

A few hours later they were headed home. It was over. Annie had slipped away to join Marisa at last. No one spoke. Guilt was creeping in around them. Had the last few days just been too much for her? She hadn't said much the past week. She had been even more withdrawn than usual. Had the threat of moving away brought on this heart attack? Who was to blame? Had Tim pushed too hard? Had Jenna been too distracted to see her failing health? Had Jake's stubbornness kept her from getting the proper care? Maybe they all were to blame. It didn't matter anymore, she was gone.

A light mist was falling the morning of the burial. There was only Jake, Jenna, Tim, Sarah Martin and her husband, a couple of neighbors that Tim didn't know and of course, Teddy. It had been a private funeral, for Annie was a private person.

Jake had requested a local bagpiper play, "Amazing Grace". The whine of the bagpipes echoed across the valley below and out through the woods. It had a haunting sound; a sound they would all long remember.

Tim's parents had sent flowers, Scottish heather with tiny pink rosebuds. Jenna took one rose from the bouquet and placed it on the base of the little stone lamb. She knew Annie would have liked that.

Chapter 9

Annie's death had changed everything. Jenna wasn't ready to tell Jake about her plans; maybe she never would now. Jake didn't seem to care about anything. One afternoon he announced, "Tim, sell anything you want. It doesn't really matter anymore."

Tim backed off completely and was preparing to go home in a few days. *I've done enough damage here*, he thought. *Jenna will be capable of caring for Jake and there is money available now if they need it.*

Tim and Jenna hadn't spent one moment alone since the morning Annie died. They couldn't seem to look each other in the eye anymore. She'd been spending more time with Dr. Davis and Tim guessed he had just met her at the wrong time and place. It wasn't meant to be.

*   *   *

The morning that Tim was to leave, Jenna showed up early to fix breakfast for him and Jake. She wanted to say her good-byes, but didn't know quite where to start. They were seated at the old kitchen table, when Jake came out of his room with tears in his eyes.

"What is it Jake?" Jenna asked. "Can I help?"

He was holding a small book that Jenna recognized as Annie's journal. Annie had written in it almost every day and he motioned for her to read it. "Start here," he said, "out loud, please."

Jenna's voice broke a little as she read Annie's words:

Tuesday, March 25th: Today our nephew came from Chicago. He seems like a fine young man. It stormed tonight, he and Jenna went to help Teddy with a new calf. Their laughter is like music to my old ears. It's so good to have family here again.

Thursday, March 27th: Today Timothy and Jake argued about money. It breaks my heart to hear them getting so angry at one another. We need Timothy now and he needs us too.

At that, Jenna's eyes moved to Tim's. Annie was a very wise woman.

Friday, March 28th: A man came today to decide how much our things are worth. Why don't they understand that you can't put a price on memories?

Monday, April 10th: It's a beautiful day today. It seems we're suddenly rich, I knew it all along. Money is a relative thing; we've always been rich. I saw Marisa again today, calling me from across the field.

<u>*Tuesday, April 11^{th:}*</u> (Annie's final entry) *I'm very tired today. My prayers have been answered. I'm so happy that Jenna and Timothy are falling in love; I can see it in their eyes. Maybe now he will stay, for Jake will need them both when I'm gone. I know they will take good care of him. Marisa calls for me now. I love her so.*

Jenna broke down, sobbing, unable to speak. Tim went to her and held her. She looked up at him through her tears, "She was right, you know. I am falling in love with you, Tim. Please don't leave, we need you."

"I'm not going anywhere," he announced. They pulled Jake to them and included him in their embrace.

Annie had been right about a lot of things. Tim did need them as much as they needed him. He finally understood about the house, about the antiques, about everything.

Chapter 10

It had been quite a spring. The three of them had decided the only way they could achieve their dreams for the house, was to try to work together. Jake had been open to every suggestion. He thought Jenna's plans were wonderful. Tim was even learning, slowly, to keep his mouth shut and not set Jenna off. There had been a few setbacks, but they were all learning to laugh again.

Tim had gone back to Chicago for a few days to end his relationship with Ellen, in person. He had called her several times in the previous weeks, trying to let her down gently. He had tried to tell her about Jenna, but the words never came. Most of the time he was talking to her answering machine, anyway.

"I'll be back in Chicago on Wednesday, and I need to talk to you. Will you meet me at my office around eleven? I'll take you to lunch," he told her, trying to sound upbeat.

"I can't wait! I've missed you so much, Tim. I know you think I can't make a single decision on my own, but honey, these past few weeks without you, have made me realize that I have to learn to stand on my own. I promise I'll do better about that," Ellen stated, excited that Tim was coming home at last.

The drive to Chicago was long and Tim practiced what he was going to say to Ellen.

"Ellen, I've found someone else."

"Ellen, you're a wonderful woman, but I don't love you."

"Ellen, get a life!"

"Ellen, you know how much I care about you, but you need to grow as a person before we can have a lasting relationship." *Hey that sounds pretty good*, Tim thought.

The next day Tim was cleaning out his desk when she walked into his office.

"Oh, Tim, I'm so glad you're home. I've really missed you!" She threw her arms around him and kissed him.

"I've missed you, too," Tim said, without looking into her eyes. *I'll tell her at lunch,* he thought. *I can't tell her here, she'll cry and the whole office will see her.*

"What are you doing to your desk?" she asked, suddenly noticing the box he was filling.

"I'm going back to Missouri to help Jake fix up his old house. I can sell real estate anywhere."

Ellen was stunned. She just stood there, trying to comprehend what he was saying.

"But I need you to be here," she said, her eyes starting to glisten with tears. "I need you to be with me. I can't be here alone. I need your strength. I need to be able to talk to you everyday, not just once in a while. I just took on a new job, I can't get off work long enough to go to Missouri. It's too far. You can't go!"

"Ellen, you don't need me; you just think you do. The only person you need is you. Quit depending on others to fill your life. Go out and fill it yourself." *I do sound like a therapist*, he thought

64

suddenly. "Go out and find new friends, get some new clothes, get a cat. You don't need me."

"Get a cat?" Ellen snapped. "After all this time together, you tell me to get a cat. Thanks, Tim, maybe you're right! I don't need you!" She turned and walked toward the door.

"I'm sorry, Ellen. I'm just not what you need. I never was." Tim walked over to her and held her. "I'm sorry, but my life has moved on and yours will too, if you'll let it. Don't be so insecure. You're beautiful, smart and talented. The world is out there waiting for you. Go after it!" He kissed the top of her head, like he would a child.

"Good-bye, Tim," she said as she closed the door.

Tim moved back to Missouri with the intention of getting his realtor's license there. His parents hated to have him move, but they saw a new side to him; more patient, more understanding, more content. They promised to come and visit and were anxious to see the old house. They couldn't wait to meet Jenna. Something told them that Jenna Adams had a lot to do with the "new" Tim.

*   *   *

A lot had been accomplished at the house, but it was never fast enough for Jenna. She was impatient, always having to wait on something. Starting a business meant lots of red tape; licensing, zoning, plumbing codes, smoke alarms, insurance. Every day was a new challenge. Sarah Martin had given Jenna lots of time off and was helping her with the business decisions. They set up a bookkeeping system and talked to contractors. Jenna carried a notepad and was constantly making lists.

The bank was calling them again for money and in early May, they had to hold the auction in the carriage house. The Amish, from the community of nearby Dansville, were the most interested in bidding and they turned out in droves. A sea of men stood outside in straw hats, black trousers and blue shirts. They seemed so stern with their serious faces, but as Tim talked with them, he realized that they were soft-spoken, gentle people.

Their horses and buggies were tied along the fences. Tim had never been around the Amish before and was fascinated by everything they said and did. Before the day was over, he had a great respect for them. With Jake's approval, he had made a deal with Seth Miller to have one carriage and one wagon restored, in exchange for the lumber of three old outbuildings, which Seth and his family would come and take down. Another group was coming in June to repair the barn roof in exchange for twenty tall, straight walnut trees in the grove behind the cattle shed. Tim felt like an old horse trader.

It was an interesting day and even Jake was enjoying it. He was proud that he had made a deal on his own. Late that afternoon, three of the Amish men hitched their horses together and, with several others muscle power, brought an old cupola up to the house from the pasture. Jenna had mentioned a few weeks earlier that she wished it could be moved to the garden and made into a gazebo. It had blown off an old barn years earlier and landed in the pasture. Now Jake presented it to her, like a housewarming gift.

She was thrilled. It was an octagon shape, badly in need of repair, with "gingerbread" trim and a sharp peaked roof with a weathervane. She knew exactly where she wanted it. "Right there on top of that big tangle of weeds," she yelled as she pointed to the spot.

The men maneuvered the horses around like pros, but Jenna tried even the gentle Amish men's patience when she yelled, "No, a little to the right. No, I mean my right. No, No, backwards. Turn it around. The other side looks better." *Turn it around?* Jenna had no concept of what that meant. The men worked another hour, unhitching and hitching the horses to get the new gazebo just right.

Jake's original deal was for one Angus steer in exchange for bringing in the cupola, but he felt sorry for the men having to work for Jenna and ended up giving them a calf, besides.

The last of the Amish men waved goodbye a little after 5:00 p.m. They wanted to get home before dark, because the buggies were dangerous on the highway at night. They had promised to return in a few weeks.

The auctioneer was happy with the sale and there would be more than enough money to take care of the bank, at least for now.

Tim, Jenna and Jake walked toward the house. It had been a very long day. Teddy stood alone in the doorway of the carriage house. It was almost empty now, just the wagons to be restored and a few odds and ends. He gave a big sigh. Teddy had lived among the leather and tack for so many years, they were like old friends. The rows of wagon wheels were gone now, Annie was gone, and he seemed to be losing everything. Teddy felt very alone.

Jenna turned to wave goodnight and saw him standing in the doorway. She went back to see if he was alright. "Teddy, why don't you come up to the house and have supper with us?" she asked.

He shook his head.

"I know we're making lots of changes around here. I promise it's going to be wonderful when it's all done. We're going to fix up your loft next. The steps won't be so steep anymore and we'll make it handier for you. You can even help me pick out the new sink and shower stall tomorrow."

"Okay," he said as he started for the stairs.

"What's wrong, Teddy? You can tell me."

"Nothin'."

"I know there's something," she insisted.

"I miss Annie as much as you do," he declared. "I loved her as much as Jake ever did."

Jenna was surprised by his statement. Teddy had never said much about his feelings. "We all loved her, but I know she wouldn't want us to be sad. She's in a better place," Jenna added.

"I know." Teddy turned and went slowly up the steps to his loft. "'Night, Jenna."

"Goodnight, Teddy."

Teddy had come to work for the McConnells at the age of 28. He grew up nearby in the small town of Voss. With no family in the area, Teddy had traveled around working for farmers and ranchers. He even drove cattle for awhile in Kansas and Oklahoma. It was a lonely existence, and he found himself back in the area he'd grown up in.   With the experience he'd gained riding the cattle trails, the McConnells hired him as their foreman.   He knew how to handle livestock and people.   He was the boss and the other hands liked and respected him, in spite of the fact he was younger than most of them. Jake's grandfather was in charge of everything when Teddy started to work there.   Jake and his father were more interested in traveling and entertaining and Teddy didn't see them except from a distance.

Jake and Annie had just married and because Annie was sort of an outsider, she often wandered through the gardens alone.   She was quiet and withdrawn.   The neighbors and guests at the house thought she was snobbish and unfriendly, but in reality she was just very shy and lonely.   She had met Jake at her father's home in St. Louis.   Both were involved with the railroad.   Annie's father knew that Jake had money and pushed her into marrying him as soon as possible.   She wasn't an outgoing person, and her father was afraid she might never marry.   Annie, raised to do as she was told, married Jake without love.

They   moved   into   the   huge   house   with   his   parents   and grandparents.   Jake's mother ruled the house with an iron hand. Annie was not to change anything, not to fix food, not to clean, wash, sew or speak socially with the servants. "It just wouldn't be proper." Annie had no friends, and the only one who ever spoke to her, other than a short greeting was Jake.

They   all   lived   together   in   the   big   old   house,   entertaining, traveling, enjoying the good life.   Everyone except Annie.   She hated parties, despised traveling and was bored and lonely most of the time. Jake treated her like a china doll; something to look at and admire from a distance, but too fragile to embrace. She felt as though she had been set on a shelf with nothing to do.

The beautiful gardens had become her paradise, her refuge from the overbearing family. She was allowed to gather flowers and water the plants if she didn't get dirty and always wore her wide-brimmed hat. "Ladies should never get burned by the sun!" Jake's mother would tell her. It was the servants' job to tend the gardens, but Annie spent as much time there as her mother-in-law would allow.

One warm summer evening, Annie slipped quietly out of the house after dinner and walked in the moonlight through the gardens. Jake and his father were entertaining some local businessmen and she was told to leave them with their cigars and brandy, to talk politics.

She stood there breathing in the warm summer scents, when suddenly Teddy appeared from nowhere. "Good evenin', Mrs. McConnell. Did I scare ya'?"

"A little," Annie said quietly.

"Sorry, it's just such a perty night, I decided to go fer a walk. I saw ya' out here. Hope it's proper fer me to talk to ya'?"

"It's fine. You're Theodore Johnson, aren't you?" Annie asked.

"Yeah, but everybody calls me Teddy, Mrs. McConnell."

"I'm Annabelle. Mrs. McConnell is my mother-in-law." They both laughed at that. They walked along the path, fireflies twinkling around them.

"Ya' know, I used to sleep out under the stars on cattle drives. Nothin' better on a warm night." They stopped and looked up at the beautiful black velvet sky with its diamonds sprinkled everywhere.

They stood there for a long while, watching the stars in silence, enjoying every moment. Alone, but no longer lonely.

That summer found them in the garden quite often, laughing and talking, or just strolling along the paths. They were content to be in each other's company.

Early one morning as she tended the roses, Annie saw Teddy ride up from the creek toward the servant quarters. She went to find him to show him the beautiful perfect yellow rose she'd found. He was waiting for her behind the little stone cottage. She looked beautiful that morning in her long filmy dress and straw hat, carrying the little basket of flowers. He leaned down from his horse to smell the rose that she held up to him. She was so tiny, so lovely that morning; he bent down to kiss her. She retreated, and he quickly got down from the horse to catch her.

"I'm sorry; I just couldn't help it," he said sadly as he pulled her into his arms. They both knew it was wrong. They knew it could never happen again. They clung to each other for a few moments, not wanting to let go. Without saying a word, Annie turned and went to the house. There on the ground, lay the perfect rose. Teddy picked it up gently.

He looked at it now, so many years later, in his old loft above the carriage house. He wished things could have been different.

Chapter 11

The students from the agriculture school had arrived, eager to start on the gardens and orchards. Jenna's visit to the school had been welcomed and they were glad for the hands-on learning opportunity. Curt, Tom, Trent, Keri and Samantha came early one Monday morning. They were like a sudden shock of electricity. The old house would never be the same.

Jenna and Tim had cleaned out two rooms upstairs to accommodate them. They left their luggage in their rooms, and went out to look at what would become the gardens. Jenna went with them, sketches in hand. She told them what she had planned and approximately the areas she wanted cleaned out. After an hour or more, she went back to her work in the old pantry and let the experts take over. Two instructors had arrived and were supervising the plans. They would stop back out from time to time over the next few weeks to see how things were going.

The crocus, jonquils and tulips had already bloomed and disappeared for the year. Jenna wanted the bulbs left where they were, just divided and thinned out a little. Daisies, roses, iris and hollyhocks were everywhere, mostly under the tangled weeds and underbrush that had taken over. Ferns were spreading over the grounds anywhere there was a shady spot. The place had definitely gone back to nature.

Teddy helped identify the brick and stone paths as the students marked the way with tiny orange flags. They scraped, dug, pushed, raked and clawed in the dirt all day and by five o'clock they had uncovered all the pathways. Some of the stepping stones and a few bricks would have to be replaced, but the rest of it was charming, just the way it was.

Jenna went out often to check their progress. At noon she took out sandwiches, drinks and a plate of brownies. Trent had brought along a radio and music was blaring from the CD player. The young students were laughing and dancing every time they took a break. Jake couldn't imagine where they got all their energy. The radio blared and the brownies disappeared.

That evening after supper, Jake showed the students around the old house and even took them to the cellar and a secret room in the back, under the solarium floor. "My great-grandfather helped hide slaves for the Underground Railroad. Quakers in the area hid the slaves under the false bottoms in their wagons of dry goods and supplies. They'd stop by, supposedly to leave off the supplies, but would move the slaves from the wagons, through the solarium and under the large plant stand to this hollowed out room below. They'd slide the plant stand to the side, crawl under the floor and their Quaker friends would move back the stand and cover the scratched areas on the dirt floor. There would be no sign of entry. This was a dangerous business."

Behind some boxes in the cellar, there was a crawl space to the secret room. "The servants of the house," Jake pointed out, "were not slaves. They took food to the entrance each day, until the next Quaker wagon came from the North to collect the people. The little room could hold three or four at a time. Many of the neighbors had similar hiding places." Jake was a storyteller, and the students listened closely with great interest.

"My family sold horses and mules to both the North and South, but no one ever suspected them of harboring slaves. One day a rebel general and some troops were in the barn buying horses, while two slaves hid in this underground room." Jake was proud of his family's involvement. "The punishment for harboring slaves was 'death by hanging'".

Jake loved to tell his stories of the past and Jenna noticed that the students were fascinated with the house and Jake. Suddenly she had a flash of genius. *Jake could be a tour guide for the guests at the Inn. I could schedule a time each day for a tour of the house and grounds, with Jake telling his stories.*

He'd love it. Jenna thought to herself. *If a walking tour was too much for him some days, he could tell stories in the library by the fireplace in the winter or in the garden during the summer. Maybe we could charge $2 or $3 for the tour?* Jenna had all the bases covered.

The next few days went by quickly. The students were a pleasure to be around. They worked hard each day and played hard each night. The garden was really beginning to take shape. Keri and Samantha had uncovered some small statues of children in the underbrush. They were strategically placed throughout the gardens. There was a stone base and a long stone slab, probably from the old quarry. Tom and Curt drug it near the old weeping willow and set it up as a garden bench. Flowers that needed to be removed, were carefully dug up and transplanted elsewhere. *By next year at this time, the gardens will be a showplace,* Jenna thought.

Ivy grew up the entire east side of the house, covering the brick. For some reason the brick had been painted white only on that side, years before. The old cracking white paint made a beautiful background for the lush green ivy that would turn crimson in the fall. The boys trimmed the ivy away from the windows and shutters, which Tim repaired and painted.

The gazebo was Tim's next project. He hammered, fixed and replaced pieces for three days before he could start painting. Jenna loved it. She planned to hang baskets of ferns from the rafters. Tim had an electrician put in underground wiring so that there could be a ceiling fan and some lighting. The gazebo was going to be the centerpiece for the beautiful gardens, and Tim was beginning to get enthused. Jenna's excitement about the Inn was infectious.

She brought him cold lemonade as he painted the old cupola. He sat down in the shade to cool off and she rubbed his tired shoulders. "And what nice shoulders they are, too," Jenna said as she massaged the knots in his back. Tim thought the lemonade and shade would cool him off, but Jenna was causing a sudden rush of heat. He pulled her onto his lap and kissed her neck. Curt whistled at them from across the yard.

"We'd better get back to work!" Jenna said with a smile.

"Yes, dear," Tim growled, but he really didn't mind. He was enjoying himself and working outside was wonderful. He wasn't a professional carpenter by any stretch of the imagination, but he was having fun. *My tired muscles and bruised body are only a small sacrifice for the common goal,* he thought with a grin. He grabbed Jenna for one last kiss and went back to work. Jenna wondered why she was getting wolf whistles and laughs as she walked back to the house carrying the lemonade tray. Maybe it was Tim's white hand print on the seat of her pants.

Gus the dog liked to be where the action was. Wherever Tim or the students were, Gus was too. Especially where they had been digging fresh dirt. Gus had bent over lots of transplanted flowers and had been scolded over and over, but it didn't do any good. Finally Jenna laid his favorite old rug on the floor of the gazebo and Gus had found his new home. He lay there watching from dawn until dusk. He was the king of his domain.

Tom, the only quiet one in the bunch, had drawn up a blueprint of the garden. He designed a geometric pattern of flowers fanning out from all eight sides of the gazebo. Jenna decided which type and color of flowers to use. The students planted for days, carefully following the diagrams. They added miniature Japanese maples and flowering cherry trees, azaleas, hostas and groundcovers. Coke cans in hand and Gus the dog looking on, the little group stood back at the end of each day to admire their work.

In three weeks they had the gardens and trees done from the house all the way to the guest cottage on the edge of the woods. It was enchanting.

The little stone cottage was such a mess, but the possibilities for something really special could be seen by everyone. Instead of going home for the weekend as usual, the students volunteered to stay and clean out the little house. Early Saturday morning armed with brooms, buckets, rubber gloves and disinfectants, they started cleaning. The radio blared and the dust flew. By Sunday evening it was clean and the entire inside, whitewashed. They had caulked the windows and painted the trim. The old Dutch door had been taken to the carriage house where Tim painted and repaired it.

They were proud of their work and came into the house to get Jenna. They dragged her out to the cottage, where Jake was already sitting in the old lawn chair where he'd been most of the day. They welcomed her in, grinning from ear to ear.

It looked great and smelled clean and fresh. It was going to be fun to decorate and Jenna could hardly wait. She hugged them all and announced, "Let's burn all this old junk and lumber and have a wiener roast."

At dusk they all sat around the fire with hot dogs and beer, singing old camp songs and telling ghost stories like a bunch of little kids. They even roasted marshmallows. Jake and Teddy sang along, too, and Tim laughed until he cried. Jenna shook her head and said, "What a bunch!"

The stars twinkled down on the little group as the moon spread its light across the new garden. *It's going to be beautiful someday,* Jenna thought.

The next week went by too quickly. The students had to get back for finals. They trimmed the orchard and tamed the grape arbors. It was the wrong time of the year for pruning, so they promised to come back in the fall to finish up. They fertilized and manicured the front lawn, tore out the plants and bushes around the pond in front of the house and appropriately planted weeping willows around the edge. They'd landscape along the front of the house when they returned in the fall.

It was hard to say goodbye to them. They'd done a wonderful job and had learned a lot in the process.

The house seemed so quiet that evening without them, even Jake didn't have much to say. He had gotten very close to Trent and Curt. They were both history buffs and hung on every word that Jake said. They enjoyed his rambling stories and stayed up late each night listening with interest. They didn't treat him like a silly, old man lost in the past. With their encouragement, Jake seemed to remember more and more and even started writing down some of the stories so he wouldn't forget them.

"You should write a book, Jake," Curt told him. "I'd buy it!"

Tom's family raised cattle in Texas and he and Teddy became pals after only two days. They had spent hours leaning on the fence talking about feed and beef prices.

Samantha and Keri followed Tim and Jenna everywhere, asking a million questions about the house and how they planned to decorate it. They couldn't wait to come back in the fall.

Keri was a fitness freak and insisted that everyone do at least fifty sit-ups each morning. That had lasted for only three days. After that, everyone threw things at her at the mere mention of "sit-ups".

Samantha was not quite five feet tall, but was able to lift her own weight in garden supplies and work rings around the three guys. They nicknamed her "Mighty Mouse," or "Mouse" for short.

*   *   *

The day after they left, the little cottage seemed to beckon Tim and Jenna to start remodeling. The contractors were already working in the house, but Tim asked them to stop what they were doing and put a bathroom in the little cottage. He knew Jenna could hardly wait to start on it. In one corner, they partitioned off the bath and put in a small hot tub for two.

The electrician put a ceiling fan from the rafters of the main room and the plumber put a small wet bar near the door. Tim cleaned out the old stone fireplace that went up through the center of the room.

Tim and Jenna cleaned up the brass on the old bed upstairs and drug it out to the cottage. They had taken all the big goose down mattresses to a professional cleaner. Now, Tim brought one of the fluffiest out to where Jenna was vacuuming the front of the fireplace.

Tim was struggling to get the mattress through the door when she came out to help. They threw it onto the bed and fell into it.

"Maybe we should break in this beautiful new bed before the newlyweds flatten out all the fluff?" Tim hinted. Jenna giggled and prayed that none of the workers in the house could see them.

"We really don't have time for this, you know," Jenna pleaded, but the look on her face suggested she might take time. He kissed her and thought how beautiful she looked with a smudge of dirt on her cheek and love in her eyes.

It wasn't the first time they'd spent an afternoon alone together. Every once in a while they'd slip away for an hour or two. They weren't fooling anyone, though, for it had been a constant source of conversation for the students. Tim and Jenna would go into town for supplies, only to return with one paint brush, giggling and grinning. The college kids got a big kick out of it. Even Jake and Teddy knew what was going on.

Jenna had decorated the guest house in dark green and white with wicker furniture and lots of ferns. Now the beautiful little house was complete.

"You know, we could have weddings in the garden and then the groom could carry the bride off to their little honeymoon cottage in the woods," Jenna told Tim as they leaned over the bottom section of the old Dutch door.

"Woman, you are a hopeless romantic, but, I love you anyway!" It was the first time he ever mentioned love.

Chapter 12

The house looked like a disaster area. The contractors were tearing everything apart and there was plaster everywhere. Tears came to Jake's eyes every time he came through the house. It was one thing to change the garden and grounds, but the house was a different story altogether. Every time Jenna started on another room, Jake shuddered. He'd spent sixty years forbidding Annie to move anything from its time-honored space. Now, he suddenly didn't know where anything was, but he knew in his heart, things had to change if Jenna's plan was going to work.

They boxed up items that couldn't be used for the Inn, marking and cataloging each item. The boxes were taken to the carriage house to go to the auction. Jenna knew it was painful for Jake. Each item that went into a box was like losing a little piece of himself, so she kept him occupied outside as much as possible.

The Amish had returned to repair the round barn roof and Seth Miller's family came to tear down several old rickety outbuildings. Jake and Teddy took their lawn chairs out to watch. It was quite a sight as they sat and pulled nails from the boards with the younger members of Seth's family. The children wore their little straw hats and overalls, their tiny bare feet carefully avoiding the rusty nails on the ground. The older children stacked the boards on hayracks while their elders crawled along the beams, trying to save whatever good lumber they could.

The men roofing the barn had found an old sleigh in the rafters and Seth had agreed to take it, the carriage and a wagon home to restore, before the Inn was to open. *Carriage and sleigh rides will be fun for the guests*, Jenna thought.

Summer was bearing down full force now and Tim was trying to get as much work done outside during the cool mornings as he could. He'd been painting the cattle shed and the trim on the barn and carriage house. He'd never worked this hard in his life. The sun had turned his body a deep tan and his copper blonde hair was bleached nearly white.

Jenna watched him from the house as he climbed the ladder, his bare back glistening in the heat. The city boy was enjoying the country life and Jenna was enjoying the view. Working toward the same goal had mellowed them both. They loved each other's company and could work side by side for hours without having to say a word. But once in a while, Tim could still set Jenna off. "You missed a spot!" Tim said, as she tried to help him paint. She slammed down the brush and went to the house. Tim just grinned.

He had gotten his Missouri realtor's license and had started to work afternoons for a small agency in Blakesburg. "Someday I'll open my own business like the one in Chicago, but not now," he told Jenna. He was committed to making the Inn a reality, but he needed a commission soon. He had been putting all of his own money into the house repairs. Jenna didn't know it, but Tim had already used most of his savings. He didn't want Jake to have to sell anymore antiques just yet.

While the men worked outside, Jenna spent her time cleaning up after the contractors. The plumbers and electricians were finished, but the carpenters were taking out a wall between two bedrooms for the suite. They were also putting in new windows and all new glass panes in the solarium. Bricklayers were redoing mortar and replacing some of the brick. They reset the wrought iron terraces above the verandah and a huge crane came to put a new water tank on the roof. "No more brown water!" Tim laughed.

Things would go along smoothly for a few days, and then there would be some sort of catastrophe. One thing always led to another. What originally seemed like a simple task would turn into a monumental project. Sun rot on the window sill led to all new woodwork in the hallway. Frayed wiring meant days of threading new wire through walls, ceilings and floors. Dust from refinishing the hardwood floors meant weeks of cleaning and dusting all the antiques and books. It was a hot, back-breaking job.

Jenna had completely quit working for Sarah now, and she missed the little store and the friendly customers. She hadn't seen any of her friends in months. She was exhausted. Every night when she went home to her apartment, there were messages from Dr. Davis. She'd sit down to read her mail and listen to the answering machine. "'Beep', Jenna I miss you, call me! 'Beep' Miss Adams, this is Dr. Davis' receptionist, he would like for you to call him. 'Beep' Jenna, where are you? 'Beep'. I want to make plans for the weekend so call me! 'Beep' Jenna are you alright? 'Beep' Why are you doing this? Is that guy staying at Jake's?"

She had gone to dinner with Chuck twice in the past month, only because he had insisted she go. She wanted to tell him about Tim, but it never seemed right. Tim was upset when she told him she was going out with Chuck. "I told Ellen that it was over, so why is it so hard for you to tell the good doctor? Or, isn't it over between you?"

"Tim, you just don't understand. I'm intimidated by him. He turns everything I say around. I've tried to explain the situation, but he only hears what he wants to hear. I'll tell him, I promise. I just don't have the time or energy to fight with him about it right now."

Tim was pulling her one way and Chuck the other. *I love Tim, but why can't I tell Chuck goodbye? Now they're both angry with me.*

Messages from Chuck, always four or five a day, each one getting more frustrated with her. She was too tired to return them; too tired to try to explain that it was over between them. It was easier just to ignore him. She'd call him tomorrow or next week. She was just too tired. One day, the messages stopped.

*   *   *

Tim and Jenna often ended their busy day with a beer and sandwich at the little roadhouse near town. One late summer afternoon as they opened the door, the bartender greeted them and motioned for them to sit at the bar.

"What can I get you folks?" he asked. "I haven't seen you around lately." He lowered his voice, "Dr. Davis is over at that table about three sheets to the wind, if you know what I mean. He's been asking everyone about you two. I don't want any trouble in here."

"There won't be any trouble," Tim announced. "Give us each a beer. We'll be over at the doctor's table." He took Jenna by the hand and went directly to Chuck's table. She didn't like the idea, but he firmly pulled her along beside him.

"Good evening, doctor," Tim said politely. "I hear you've been asking around about us. What is it you'd like to know?"

"Tim, please don't do this," Jenna begged.

"I want to know why Jenna is spending so damn much time with you and that old man, McConnell. If it's money you want honey, I've got plenty. Haven't I always spent money on you? I've always bought you nice stuff, took you nice places? What do you want from me?" he asked as he tried to get up from his chair.

"She doesn't want anything from you, Doc. Don't you get that? She doesn't want anything." Tim repeated, as he pushed Chuck back into his chair. "Go home and sober up, Doc, before you embarrass yourself anymore than you already have."

Tim grabbed Jenna by the arm and marched her to the door. "Cancel those beers. We'll be back another day," he announced to the bartender.

Outside, Jenna was furious. "Was that absolutely necessary?" she asked, hands on her hips.

"Yeah, I think it was!"

Neither of them spoke on the drive home, or for several days, as it turned out.

*   *   *

Summer was nearly over when the carpenters finished. Jenna was glad to have the house to herself again. The noise of the hammers and drills had finally ceased and she was enjoying the quiet. She stood at the kitchen sink cleaning raspberries for supper. She was trying to make more balanced meals for Jake. His diabetes was much better with all her attention, and the close supervision of his insulin. His mind was clearer now and he seemed happier.

She looked across the brick patio and out to the gardens. She wished Keri and Samantha were here to see it. The flowers were spectacular in the late afternoon sun. Long shadows spread out across the yard in gorgeous shades of green, beckoning her to come out and sit for awhile. She wanted to, but there was so much left to do. She vowed that next summer, she'd pick fresh bouquets every morning for the breakfast table and she'd sit in the gazebo to visit with her guests each afternoon. But, not today, today she had to keep going. It was almost September and Jenna hoped to open the Inn by Thanksgiving.

Chapter 13

Fall college classes had started again and the ag students were coming for Labor Day weekend and would stay two weeks this time. Jenna and Tim worked night and day to finish the bedrooms for the kids. They would be so surprised to see how much work had been completed in the old house. Everyone was looking forward to their return, especially Jake. Having the young people around with all their energy and enthusiasm kept him feeling young and gave him something to look forward to. They loved his stories and Jenna only hoped his tours with the guests would give him as much pleasure when the Inn finally opened.

Tim and Jenna had carefully decorated the first two bedrooms with antique four-poster beds and lace curtains. Each of the six bedrooms had its own fireplace and Jenna decided that each room should contain a collection of antiques that would go along with the room's theme and color scheme.

One room housed the porcelain doll collection. Another held dozens of neatly folded quilts and Battenberg pillows. There was a large carousel horse in the corner of one room, so Jenna put up old circus posters she'd found in the attic and displayed all the carousel music boxes on the mantle. A floppy antique clown sat atop the trunk at the foot of the bed. Each room had its own personality and though some things were fresh and new, the antiques added a certain warmth and charm.

Down the hall in the old nursery, Jenna filled a small cradle with ferns, put a teddy bear collection on the window seat and used a large dollhouse as the base for the bedside table. A beautiful christening gown was hung on the wall in a place of honor. She named this room, "Marisa's Room".

Wonderful pieces of furniture were everywhere. It was like having her very own antique store to choose from. She selected brass beds, canopies and daybeds, each one unique it its own way. Chairs, dressers, wardrobes and candle stands were placed everywhere needed.

The Raggedy Ann collection that had been Annie's very own was tucked in here and there. Band boxes, rocking horses and feathery old hats were set on dressers or hung over chairs. "Jenna, you have a real talent for putting ordinary things together and making them look extraordinary," Sarah had told her on more than one occasion.

*   *   *

"Tim, help me open the windows. I want to let in lots of fresh air for the kids to enjoy," Jenna yelled from across the hall.

Just then, Tim heard their van drive up. "They're here!"

Both he and Jenna were exhausted and were looking forward to Labor Day weekend with the kids. They'd take a couple of days off before they set to work finishing the landscaping. Tim needed rest, and after a tour of the guest cottage, the gardens and the entire second floor, they all sat down in the gazebo. It was time to catch up on all the news. They all started talking at once. So much had changed over the summer. It was a wonderful transformation. Now they could all see what had been only in Jenna's imagination. "It's truly starting to look like an inn. I love it all!" Keri announced.

Sunday morning dawned a warm and sunny day. Jenna had packed a picnic lunch and made arrangements for them all to go horseback riding at Doc Thompson's stables. Tim and Jenna had been with Doc quite a lot that summer, making plans for the horse show and trail rides. He had lots of ideas and planned to promote the Inn as the perfect place to stay for his clients who boarded horses.

Today, Doc came hurrying out to greet them. "Jenna, Chuck Davis is in the stable. He's been drinking. I just wanted to warn you."

"Oh, no!" Jenna replied. She led the way around to the back where Doc had the horses saddled up and ready to go. Maybe she could avoid Chuck, but no, there he was.

"Jen, where have you been? I've left a hundred messages on your machine. Why didn't you call me back?" Chuck asked with a slurred voice.

"Glad you're not doing surgery this morning, Chuck!" Tim said under his breath.

"I've been working at Jake's," Jenna announced, embarrassed that their friends had to see this.

"You're always at Jake's. I thought you'd put him in a home by now!"

Tim grabbed her as she went for Chuck. "I'll bet you did! Well, I haven't and I'm not going to!" she shouted, trying to loosen Tim's grip.

"Why don't you let this guy, what's his name, take care of Jake? You don't owe them anything; you're not his family!"

"That's it!" Tim announced as he stepped in front of Jenna. "She's going to be family when she becomes my wife," Tim grabbed Jenna again and marched her away from the good doctor.

"Your wife? You've never even mentioned marriage."

"Well, I have now!" Tim announced. "Right here in front of God and everybody!" He kissed her hard and the gang went wild. They were yelling, laughing and whistling. They were spooking the horses.

Chuck turned and walked back to the stables. Jenna felt a little sorry for him as she stood, cushioned in Tim's arms. This wasn't the way she wanted him to find out. She looked up at Tim. He was grinning down at her and all she could do was smile.

Chapter 14

The late summer sun was warm on their faces as they turned the horses south out of the woods and into the meadow. The lead horse started galloping toward the creek as Tim held on for dear life.

He had forgotten his anxiety about riding, in the excitement of the moment. He had finally asked Jenna to marry him. He hadn't planned on doing it in such a public display, but now it was up to her. They hadn't talked about it. *Maybe she isn't ready.* He knew she loved him, he just didn't know how much.

Jenna watched him as he plopped up and down in the saddle. The gentle old horse he was riding had been hand-picked by Doc, who knew Tim had never ridden before. Jenna smiled to herself as his elbows flopped along with each bump. He probably wasn't enjoying himself, but he was being a good sport and she loved him for that.

The horses carefully crossed the creek and Jenna headed for the clump of willows downstream. It was a perfect day. Keri and Samantha laid out their picnic lunch as Jenna and the boys watered the horses and tied them out to graze.

Curt asked the little group to take a vote to decide if Tim should propose properly before they ate. They insisted he get down on one knee and do it right. Keri made a ring from a dandelion stem. Tim slipped it on Jenna's finger, begging her to marry him. She finally said "yes" after much deliberation and coaxing from the audience.

After a long, lazy lunch, Tim and Jenna walked alone along the creek while the "wild bunch", as Tim called them, took turns throwing each other into the water. Jenna took off her boots and sat down on the bank with her feet dangling in the cool, clear water. She motioned for Tim to join her.

"I hope we haven't pressured you into an answer," Tim said in a serious tone. "I want you to be sure about this."

Jenna smiled and took his face into her hands. "I've never been more sure of anything in my life!"

*   *   *

As beautiful as the dandelion ring was, it didn't hold a candle to the one he presented her at breakfast the next morning. He let her sleep in late, but he couldn't stand waiting a minute longer. He'd gone over to the store and brought back coffee and donuts.

He sat down on the edge of the bed and kissed her awake. "Good morning, Sleepyhead," he smiled. He had watched her dozing in the early morning light. She seemed so small, curled up clutching her pillow. So fragile, yet so strong in many ways.

Tim had the diamond in the glove compartment of his car. He had been afraid she'd find it somewhere in the old house and possibly throw it away by mistake, in one of her wild cleaning frenzies. It had been in his car for over two weeks now. He just hadn't found the right time to ask her. Yesterday's little run-in with Chuck had just forced the issue, and Tim was glad it had happened.

He took her hand and slipped on the diamond. It sparkled in the early morning sun. Jenna held it away from her, "Oh, Tim! It's so beautiful!"

He held her and brushed the tousled curls from her eyes. "You're beautiful." They had their coffee and donuts in bed and didn't show up at the house until after eleven.

The "wild bunch" was playing volleyball over the clothesline with an inflatable beach ball. *It doesn't take much to entertain them*, Jenna thought. Curt hollered, "Where have you two been, getting supplies?" Everyone nearly fell down laughing.

"No, getting engaged!" Tim yelled back.

Keri and Samantha rushed over to see the ring. Even Jake got up from his old lawn chair near the make-shift volleyball court to give them a hug. They called Tim's parents that evening, who seemed happy with the news. Jim and Lisa were planning to come for the opening of the Inn, and wanted to meet Jenna at last. It had been a perfect Labor Day weekend.

* * *

The next morning started out with a bang, literally. A thunderstorm woke them all up early. It looked as if it would rain most of the day, so they delayed the landscaping and decided to work in the solarium instead. Jenna envisioned it as a place for the guests to relax and soak up sunlight, especially during the colder months. Maybe it could be a place to enjoy early morning coffee, a good book in the afternoon or a warm romantic place for a candlelight supper for two. She wanted "nature, indoors."

The old stone foundation made a wall about two feet high. Combined with the river rock floor, it absorbed heat all day from the glass roof and walls above. The natural solar heat radiated all night to maintain a fairly constant temperature. It would be prefect for a variety of plants, too.

Tom and Curt raked the rock floor and smoothed it out where the contractors had worked earlier. Trent leveled the stepping stones and cleaned the old fish pool. Tim checked out the water system and made a list of supplies for the girls to pick up in town: a new recycling pump, faucets, garden hoses, goldfish and beer.

Jenna and the girls stopped first at the nursery in Blakesburg. They spent two hours there selecting ferns and large greenhouse plants, even a few potted trees. Samantha decided to start some water plants and lily pads in the fish pool. "I'll deliver everything this afternoon," the salesman said with a smile.

Jenna put the bill on her credit card and prayed it wouldn't go over her limit. She'd already maxed out two others, and was afraid to tell Tim how much she was spending. Her rent was due, but Sarah would understand, wouldn't she? No income was really starting to put a bind on the small amount of money Jenna had saved over the years. She didn't know quite how to approach the subject with Jake or Tim. She'd put in months of hard work on the house without making a dime. Money would be no problem after the auction or when the Inn opened, but until then, she'd have to be very conservative.

They got the other supplies, stopped at KFC for a bucket of chicken and headed home. Curt and Trent had placed small tables and matching wicker chairs in groupings around the solarium. Tim had opened the skylights and turned on the new ceiling fans. The sun was coming out now and the huge glass room was warming up fast. They all sat down to eat lunch.

The plants arrived, as promised, in the middle of the afternoon. With lots of plant stands from the attic and the old dry sink from the summer kitchen, the girls arranged and rearranged the truckload of plants and trees. Jenna always insisted that things look just right from every direction.

Samantha, "Mouse", was carrying a potted tree over to the southeast corner. Trent went to help her. She handed it to him, but it was too heavy and he dropped it. Everyone laughed and Keri blamed him for not doing his "sit-ups".

Jake and Teddy came in to check on the progress. "Jenna, I like the plants. Do ya' think I could learn how to take care of 'em?" Teddy asked. "I'd like to help."

"I don't see why not," Jenna answered. "Maybe Tom would show you how to water and such while he's here the next few days. He's the expert." They all nodded in agreement and Teddy was thrilled. He helped Tom hang some of the larger ferns from the skylight support.

Tim got the new pump working and the old dolphin-shaped fountain spit water down over the rocks and into the fish pool. It gave a few gurgles. "It works!" he announced and everyone cheered.

The new water plants were set into place and the goldfish were released. It looked and smelled like a little tropical paradise. "All we need now is a parrot," laughed Jake.

Chapter 15

Jenna could hardly get out of bed the next morning. Her back hurt and she was so tired. Moving the plants and furniture had been hard, heavy work. She showered in the hottest water she could stand, letting the spray pound on the sore muscles in her back. She didn't want Tim to know it, but she was wearing out. The heavy work was taking a toll on her, but she slipped into her jeans and a sweater and hurried to join the kids in the orchard.

They had been out since dawn, taming the grape arbor and pruning trees and berry bushes. They had stayed up late, laughing and talking in the new solarium with Tim and Jake. Jenna had excused herself early and went home to bed.

"Good morning, Hon," Tim said as he looked up from raking. Piles of grapevines and prickly trimmings from the raspberries were everywhere. Jenna bent down to pick some up and winced.

"Are you okay?"

"Fine," Jenna answered, not wanting anyone to know about her back.

The next several days were spent giving the front of the house a more formal look. Jenna wanted it to look more inviting to guests and passersby. The weeping willows around the pond had grown graceful over the summer and the reflection of the Inn in the water was magnificent. The large oak trees near the house shaded the front lawn and the verandah.

Tom and Curt drew up plans and went to the nursery for new shrubs and extra hostas. They bought topiary trees in large planters for either side of the front door. Jenna loved it, but wondered how she'd pay for them. Jake's cash was depleted and so was hers. The bank wouldn't lend them anymore money. This whole idea had been hers and now she felt responsible for the cost.

The soft warm autumn evenings made everyone sleepy after a hard day of work. The sound of crickets in the distance and the "whir" of the ceiling fans caused everyone to retire early, especially Jenna.

*   *   *

With two days left of their stay, the "wild bunch" finished ahead of schedule. Everything looked great, but there was one eyesore left, the fences. It was like looking at a beautiful picture through an ugly frame. As they stood in the middle of the road looking back toward the house, everyone agreed. The fences had to go. Everyone that is, except Jake. He couldn't bear to lose them, so they surrendered to the idea of restoration. Fence mending had nothing to do with horticulture classes, but it had to be done.

The next morning, hammers were pounding, saws were buzzing, music was blasting and they were at it again. Jake hobbled down the drive, lawn chair and paint brush in hand, as Gus the dog followed along behind. Jake was planning to help paint, so he sat down with Gus plopping down beside him.

Tim and Curt measured and cut new boards wherever needed, then set posts straight and nailed boards back on. The rest painted, while Jenna kept food and drinks coming and made at least four trips to town for more paint. Gus supervised and two days later they were finished; exhausted, paint smudged, sunburned, but finished. Now the beautiful picture had a gorgeous new frame. They all agreed it had been worth it. Jake beamed with pride as they stood in the road looking back. "Now this is the way I remember it!"

*   *   *

The little group had their suitcases packed but was having a hard time leaving. Tim promised them a free weekend with no work right before Thanksgiving. It would be a trial run before the opening. They would be the guinea pigs for the new chef they had just hired. Jenna wanted to take pictures before they left. She yelled, "Everyone in the garden! Now, get in front of the gazebo. Get closer! By the fish pool. Now, on the verandah. Beside the new willows. Smile, for heaven's sake!"

Sarah stopped by and Jenna had her take a picture of the kids all lined up on the new fence with herself and Tim, Jake and Teddy crouched down in front of them. When the pictures came back, all four of them had "finger, bunny ears" above their heads. Jenna wasn't surprised.

*   *   *

The next week found Tim and Jenna putting the finishing touches on the suite and its adjoining bathroom. It would be private and elegant with the long French doors opening out to the balconies above the verandah.

Across the hall from the suite was the large main bathroom that would be shared by all the other guests. It held a leaded glass cabinet that Jenna commandeered as a linen closet. She filled it with thick, fluffy, rose-colored towels and a collection of antique perfume bottles. They were the same mellow shade of rose found in the stained glass window behind the old claw foot tub. A free standing mirror stood in one corner, with a small velvet bench in front of it. There were ferns everywhere.

Jenna sat down and looked at herself in the mirror. She looked frazzled. She could see the reflection of the tub behind her. The whole room just invited her to come in for a warm bath and Jenna accepted the invitation. She pinned up her long, curly brown locks, squirmed out of her old clothes and stepped into the tub filled with bubbles.

It wasn't quite dark yet and the light of dusk lit up the stained glass window and danced the colors across the room and up the walls. It was an enchanting sight. A little cherub statue at the end of the tub smiled at her as she lay her head back and closed her eyes.

She had worked almost non-stop the last few days and she was glad that the upstairs was finally finished. Tim had been staying at her apartment while the upstairs got its facelift, and she wondered if it would be a permanent arrangement. He'd never said anything else about setting a date, so she guessed he liked things just the way they were.

Tim peeked in and saw her lying in the tub. He went downstairs and opened a bottle of wine and grabbed two glasses. Jenna opened one eye, as he walked in. Tim poured them each a glass and sat down on the gray marble floor beside her. "Ya' know," he said, "this place is growing on me. The first morning I was here, I couldn't wait to leave. Now I'm planning to stay forever. I used to think country folks were, well…Now, I'm not sure I could ever go back to city life."

Jenna reached over and lazily gave him a bubble bath mustache and beard. He put a big foam blob on her nose. She filled his shirt pocket and then smashed it against his chest. Before it was over, they were both in the tub, clothes and all.

Chapter 16

October came and went. The crisp autumn days and scarlet leaves told them that opening day was drawing near. The roadside was afire with bright orange sumac and golden trees fluttering in the brisk north wind. Fall in the Missouri hills was breathtaking.

The chef, whose name was Bob but liked being called "Roberto", helped set up the kitchen. A new stove, refrigerator/freezer and sink were installed. Jenna had scraped the contact paper off the glass cupboard doors and Roberto arranged them the way he wanted. Gleaming white French bake ware showed through the glass, with rows and rows of colorful tins containing cocoas, baking powder, spices and herbs. Large copper bowls and silver serving trays set atop the crisp white paper-lined shelves. An old butcher block table from the cellar set in the middle of the floor and Tim hung a big copper pot hanger above it. Roberto brought his own pots and utensils to hang there and planted an herb garden in clay pots along the window sills.

Tim placed a soda fountain table and four chairs in the corner. Jenna hung copper molds and dried herb bunches everywhere and filled several odd-sized canning jars with pastas to set on the counter. She'd just put something down and Roberto would move it. Sometimes only an inch, but he moved it just the same.

This was going to be <u>his</u> kitchen and he wanted Jenna to know it. She was afraid their personalities were not compatible, but after tasting the pastries he brought from the oven, she decided she would just stay out of his way.

The den and entryway were Tim's October projects. The walls in both rooms were paneled in a warm oak. Tim cleaned and polished everything, even all the grooves in the large roll top desk. Jenna tore down the heavy drapes and let the sun stream in.

The books fascinated Tim the most. Jake helped him sort and clean. They boxed up lots of memorabilia and a cigar box collection. The big overstuffed leather furniture was indestructible and only needed a good cleaning. Tim brought down a big bear skin rug to put in front of the fireplace and a couple of safari mounted heads for the walls. *This is a "man's room"*, he thought. *No lace and ruffles here!*

Jenna brought in a tray of coffee and Roberto's latest pastry creation. She gasped when she saw the bear's entire head attached to the rug. "Where did you find that disgusting thing?" she asked bluntly.

"In the attic, next to these," Tim proudly pointed to the animal heads on the wall.

"Oh Lord, help us all." She pleaded with him to take them down, but a democratic vote was taken, two to one. Jenna lost and the bear stayed. She set down the tray and backed out of the room, pretending that the animals were stalking her.

* * *

The entry hall was paneled and large tapestries and mirrors hung on both sides leading to the stairs. A magnificent chandelier hung from the ceiling and now that it had been cleaned and all the bulbs replaced, the beauty showed again, as it must have years before.

Tim and Teddy removed all the statues. "That many nude people in a hallway make me nervous," Tim had announced.

Jenna laughed and said, "You just don't appreciate fine art." But she was glad the statues were gone, too. The entryway seemed twice as big and much brighter. Tim had cleaned the wood with warm almond oil, a concoction Jake's mother had used years before. It smelled wonderful.

The entire north side of the house looked out into the woods and away from the other buildings. There was a long, narrow sitting room, a large storage area and the old summer kitchen that was screened in and accessible from the outdoors. There wasn't going to be time now to redecorate this side, so they closed it off, to work on when time permitted.

The old parlor was an antique lover's dream come true. Two floor to ceiling French doors opened to the verandah. Jenna ripped down the dusty old blue velvet drapes and let in sunshine for the first time in years. In one corner was a gray velvet couch. Two matching wing chairs sat near the fireplace and a beautiful mahogany side table sat between them, inviting conversation and coffee by the fire.

Jenna had spent all week stripping the wainscoting and chair rails in the dining room. The beautiful grain of the wood came back as she went along. She wanted to strip off the wallpaper, too. It looked as if it would peel right off. She started at the edge of one loose seam and ripped upwards; nearly half the wall came off in one piece. Underneath was a real surprise.

"Tim, Jake, come here quick!" Jenna shrieked. "Hurry, you won't believe this!"

Tim came running and Jake shuffled as fast as he could. Tears came to the old man's eyes, as they all went to the wall to tear off more paper. There, beneath the paper, was a mural of the homestead dated by the artist in 1898. It had a simple, folk art look. The house, the round barn and carriage house looked exactly the same, with the fences and circle drive around the pond. It showed many outbuildings that weren't standing anymore.

"Look, there's the cupola on that long horse barn," Jenna said.

"There's the creek running behind the woods and through the pasture," Tim pointed out.

They went on around the room, peeling paper as they went. Two other walls were plain, but on each side of the fireplace, there were beautiful weeping willow trees cascading down the walls.

"Well," Jenna smiled, "we chose the right name." *The Inn at Willow Creek will be a wonderful place,* she thought.

Jake couldn't remember the mural and was sure that the walls had been papered even when he was a child. He was thrilled.

A set of French doors opened out into the solarium. The three of them stepped out and peered back through the glass at the glorious mural. Above the long dining room table were three suspended

Tiffany lamps in the same greens as the beautiful willows. It looked as if they'd been made especially to match the wall. Maybe they had.

With only two weeks until Thanksgiving and Opening Day, the house was nearly ready and Jenna's thoughts turned to running the Inn. She'd hired two neighbor ladies to clean "as needed". Jenna would take care of the business end and finances. Tim would keep up the maintenance and help Jenna entertain and wait on the guests. Jake was to be in charge of public relations and tours of the estate, a job which he took very seriously. Teddy would take care of the cattle and see to it that the solarium plants were tended to. The Amish farmers had returned the restored carriage, wagon and sleigh. Now Teddy would also be in charge of carriage and sleigh rides.

Roberto was more than in charge of the kitchen, he owned it (or at least he thought he did.) He was grouchy, intimidating and after a few days of putting up with his "moods", Jenna had had it. He'd yelled at Jake about moving some utensils and Jenna was too tired to put up with it anymore. She marched into the kitchen and stated frankly, "Roberto, change your attitude today or you are fired!" She walked into the dining room and pretended to count the silverware, holding her breath all the while. What if he quit? They'd never be able to find a new chef in a week.

Roberto slowly peeked around the corner, "I'm sorry, Miss Adams, but I need to know where everything is at all times."

"What you need to know 'at all times' is that Jake owns this house and lives here. It's his kitchen, not yours. We all need to get along if we're going to work together. Now, let's sit down and make some decisions about our menu."

That's all it took. They had reached an understanding of sorts. Jenna would respect his territory, but he would respect her authority. They sat in the kitchen, plotting and planning, listening to each other's ideas.

Jenna had hoped to have a certain dish that would become associated with dining at the Inn at Willow Creek, something like prime rib or filet mignon. She knew it should beef. After all, the McConnell's were famous for their cattle.

"Maybe we could advertise that we raise our own beef, here at the Inn," she said getting really excited about the idea.

"What if we served Beef Wellington, baked in a pasty crust? We could serve local wines and maybe fruit desserts from our own orchard," Roberto chimed in.

Time was running out. Jenna worked around the clock for two days straight. They set up a menu for breakfast, lunch, dinner and candlelight suppers, each one using local foods, like Ozark honey-cured ham and Missouri peaches.

*   *   *

Sarah came by to help Jenna with the books before the opening and couldn't believe her eyes. "What have you been doing for money, girl?" she asked. Sarah was astonished that there was nothing left in the Inn's account.

"It's okay," Jenna informed her. "We're almost ready and the Inn will start making money in two weeks. We just have to hang on until then."

"No wonder you couldn't pay your rent. Most of the bills have been paid from your own checking account or credit card!"

"I'll be alright if you can give me a few more weeks to pay the rent. I hate it that the contractors haven't been paid, but so far they haven't complained."

"They won't complain," Sarah interrupted, "Tim paid them months ago. I saw him. You two have a lot of money tied up in this place. The Inn is a risky business, Jenna, out here in the middle of nowhere. I hope you know what you're doing."

"The auction is scheduled for December 18th. Jake will pay us back as soon as he gets his money," Jenna said, trying to sound sure of herself. Nothing was in writing. They hadn't made any formal agreements. Jenna was just going on blind faith, but she trusted Jake. *Tim must trust him, too, or he wouldn't be using his own money, either.*

It had never really occurred to Jenna that her plan might not work. She had jumped in with both feet, sure that everything would eventually just fall into place. Everything she had on earth was invested in this house; Tim and Jake, too. Everything hinged on the success of the Inn. She suddenly felt panicky. *What if it doesn't work?*

She was touched by the fact that Tim had paid the contractors. He must believe the Inn will be a success or he wouldn't have become so involved. He'd worked every bit as hard as Jenna to restore the old house. Her plan had to work, it just had to.

Jenna's back was still bothering her and she was so tired she could hardly drag herself out of bed in the mornings. Today was no different, she yawned as she worked under the stairway in the butler's pantry. She'd been making out the grocery lists and needed to consult with Roberto on the rest. Tim had gone to town to stock the wine racks. Suddenly, the smoke detectors went off. She panicked. She ran wildly through the house to find the source. The alarms were blaring; it was deafening.

There, in the den, she found Jake trying to pry open the damper on the fireplace with a poker. "I forgot to open it!" he yelled above the alarms. Together, they released it. Jenna closed the den door to try to contain the smoke and opened windows to air it out. She and Jake went from room to room, resetting the alarms. Finally, silence, sweet silence.

"Well," Jenna sighed, "at least we know the alarms work." She put her arm around Jake. He was trembling and she realized it had really upset him. Slowly they reopened the door to the den and looked through the blue haze.

"I'm so sorry," Jake said sadly.

"It'll be fine," Jenna said, trying to sound calm. Her heart was pounding and the rush of adrenaline was giving her a headache. She put a fan blowing outward through the window and turned up the ceiling fans. She looked down at the bear on the floor. Now, not only was he ugly, he smelled bad too.

When Tim got back they surveyed the damage. The other rooms had been spared, but they still smelled of smoke. Tim opened every window and turned on all the fans. There was a wind chill factor in the hallways.

Jenna crushed up some dried herbs and lavender in the summer kitchen. She placed bowls of it in every room, hoping it would give off a natural scent and absorb the smoke. "Isn't that better?" she asked, as Tim walked in.

"It smells like a spring garden, after a forest fire!" he barked. "Put on a parka and follow me!" He mumbled something about Chicago being the "Windy City" and led the way into the den.

The haze was gone now, but black soot covered the front of the fireplace and along the mantle. Jenna picked up a book. Her hands were black. She tried to clean the cover, but it smeared. Jake tried to help but his eyes were brimming with tears and she made him sit down to rest. By two o'clock, they gave up. Tim called a professional cleaning service and the insurance company. Insurance would pay, but there was a $1,000 deductible.

The cleaners came the next morning and started wiping off each antique book. They took furniture, the bear and mounted heads outside and sprayed them with a chemical for the smell. Gus the dog growled at the bear. "I know just how you feel," Jenna said as she patted Gus's head. She sat down next to him and began to cry.

This was the last straw. Jenna broke down sobbing and couldn't stop shaking. Tim and Jake soon came around the side of the house and found her huddled by the dog. Jake brought out a blanket to put around her but it didn't help. Even Roberto seemed concerned. Tim brought the car around and carried her to the front seat. They went directly to the clinic. He called ahead and Dr. Davis met them at the door.

"Jenna, what's happened to you?"

A quick exam found the answer. "She's totally dehydrated and at the point of exhaustion. I'm putting her into the hospital for a few days," he announced. "When was the last time she ate something? She's lost 14 pounds." Tim had no idea. The doctor seemed to be blaming him. She was always seeing to it that he and Jake were eating properly, but Tim couldn't remember the last time he'd seen her eat. The strain of the last few months had finally caught up with her. Her tired body couldn't take anymore stress.

They went to the hospital, where Chuck called the nurses with strict instructions: total bed rest, no visitors, IVs, high calorie foods and absolutely no stress!

In only three days the "wild bunch" were coming for their free weekend and Thanksgiving was only a week away. The opening would just have to be postponed.

Tim called the four couples who had reservations. They weren't happy, but they understood. He also called the college and spoke to Trent, who sounded both disappointed and concerned about Jenna. Later, Tim phoned his parents who were planning to arrive Thanksgiving morning for the opening. He was drained, and his mother could hear the distress in his voice. "Sorry," he said, "I was really looking forward to seeing you."

"Us, too," she said. "Take good care of her, Tim."

Take care of her? He certainly hadn't been doing a very good job of that. Tim couldn't believe that he hadn't noticed how tired she'd become. He hadn't even noticed how much weight she'd lost. How could he be with her every day, yet not really see what was happening to her? Chuck had made Tim feel that it was all his fault.

Tim was near exhaustion himself and he was suddenly afraid that Jenna might be seriously ill. He called Jake and put him and Teddy in charge of the cleaning crew. "Just see to it that they get everything back in order before Jenna comes home." Jake was crying and felt responsible for Jenna's collapse. "I'm sure she'll be fine. She just needs some rest," Tim said, trying to reassure Jake and himself.

With the help of a little Valium, Jenna slept for almost 48 hours. The nurses were pumping her full of fluids. Tim sat in a chair beside her, dozing off. Jenna opened her eyes several times and Tim was always there, watching TV, sleeping, reading the paper or just holding her hand. *He really does love me*, Jenna thought, as she slipped back into dreamland.

Chuck stopped in two or three times a day to check on her. On the third day they started a series of tests. Jenna was groggy, but insisted that she was feeling better and needed to go home. "Well, you must be better," Chuck announced. "You sure are getting bossy." The tests came back fine and he released her the next morning. Tim went to sign her out, while the doctor sat down on the bed beside her.

"The guy adores you," Chuck announced.

"I adore him, too," Jenna said as she started to get up.

"I'm jealous, you know, and angry at myself. I didn't realize how much you meant to me, until you were gone." He helped her up and deposited her into a wheelchair.

"Chuck, I…"

"Don't say anything, Jenna. I know it's over. I've know it for a very long time. He seems like a good guy. I was prepared to hate him, but watching you two together these last few days, well, I know you belong together. Forgive me for taking you for granted. I know my career got in the way, but sometimes it just had to come first."

"Would you have stayed here in my room with me?"

"Probably not," Chuck answered honestly. He kissed her cheek and wheeled her to the front desk where Tim was waiting.

Chuck and Tim shook hands. "Take good care of her and make sure she gets some rest."

Chapter 17

"Good grief, I'm not an invalid!" Jenna protested, as Tim carried her up the stairs and plopped her on the bed in the suite.

"You're staying here for awhile," he announced. "I don't want you at the apartment alone."

Teddy and Jake hovered over her, fluffing her pillows and straightening her blankets. Sarah was there too. "I've done the laundry and the bookwork is up to date. What else can I be doing?" she asked.

"Sarah, you've done more than your share now. I think we can handle it until Jenna gets back on her feet. Thanks for everything," Tim said as he gave her a hug.

"Okay, if you're sure. I'll see you tomorrow." She gave a wave goodbye.

The three men didn't know quite how to help. Jenna got up to go the bathroom and they followed her. At the door she stopped. "Guys, I think I can handle it from here. I love you all, but BACK OFF!"

Two days later, Jenna sat curled up in the sunny solarium reading a book. The past few days had been very restful and she was beginning to feel like her old self again. Tim was still smothering her with attention and she loved him for that.

Roberto was feeding her constantly with high calorie treats, "little experiments", he called them. Streusel coffee cakes, Danish almond twists, homemade breads and muffins, all warm from the oven. "You need to try these to see if they can be served at the Inn," he insisted. Jenna knew he was just trying to fatten her up, but did as she was told. He sat with her for hours, going over recipes and lists. He was the designated baby-sitter, seeing to it that she ate and rested.

The day before Thanksgiving, Jenna napped in the suite while Jake, Tim and Teddy worked in the attic, sorting and packing boxes for the auction. Every time she dozed off, they would slide a box or drop something. She wasn't resting, so finally she went up to see what was going on.

The three men were going through old trunks and pulling out military uniforms and old gowns with hoop skirts. Jake was telling them that each Christmas that a new governor was elected, his grandfather would host a Governor's Ball. The attic was actually the ballroom.

"In the twenties, they held dances here every Saturday night. If only this house could talk," Jake remarked. "Bootleg whiskey was brought in from the Ozarks in old trucks. The local law officers could see what was going on, but knew better than to stop it. Grandfather McConnell had been responsible for getting them their jobs, and the sheriff was his best friend."

The story gave Jenna an idea. "I know how we can advertise for the new opening." She startled them. They had no idea that she had been behind them.

"You should be in bed," Tim said with a frown. He had on a Confederate hat and military sword."

"Listen, it just hit me. We could open right before Christmas with a Governor's Ball. Bob Ellington was just elected two weeks ago and Sarah knows his sister. Think of all the free publicity. We have to clean everything out of here for the auction anyway." They all looked at each other. Tim wasn't sure, but she slowly persuaded him.

"Well, if you can get the governor to come," he said. "But, we'll need some help."

"I'll help!" Jake insisted.

"Me, too!" chimed Teddy.

"I don't want you to overdo, Jenna, or we'll be right back where we started," Tim shook his finger as he spoke.

"Yes, Sir, Officer McConnell, Sir!" she saluted. "I'll use the phone by my bed to make some calls. I'll be good, I promise."

Jenna called Sarah immediately. Sarah agreed to talk to the new governor's sister and see what she could do. Next, Jenna phoned the present governor's office and spoke with his secretary. She explained the history of the Governor's Ball and made up something about helping bring a smooth transition from one administration to another. *A little public relations couldn't hurt.* The secretary checked the schedule and agreed it might work. She'd speak to the governor and get back to her.

Later, Jenna called the moving company and made arrangements for a crew and three trucks to come on Monday to remove all the extra antiques. They could take them to the auction house in St. Louis. That would give her time to clean the attic.

Sarah called to say that the new governor would be proud to attend the Ball. He thought it would be a good opportunity to mend some political fences.

By late afternoon, the plans were set for Saturday, December 23rd, exactly one month from tomorrow. The governor's office would make the announcement of the Ball as a news release from the Associated Press. By next week, the Inn would be famous.

Jenna's mind was running overtime. She'd personally call the old and new governors on Monday and invite them to spend the night of the Ball at the Inn. She'd have a press conference next week and serve the news crew lunch in the solarium. She'd have Jake tell about the house and the history of the Governor's Ball. The free publicity would be priceless.

She'd get started on cleaning the attic after the movers were done. Then, decorate for Christmas and hire a band. But, what was she going to do about money? The auction wasn't until the eighteenth and the Ball was the twenty-third. She'd have to have a serious talk with Tim. Just then, he walked in and sat down on the bed beside her. "Did you hear back from the governor's office?"

She told him all the details and some of her plans for a news conference. "You're a genius, but this will mean a lot of work. Do you think you're up to it?" Tim asked as he put his arms around her.

"I'll be fine, I promise. I'll pace myself this time. We'll let the movers finish the packing and do the heavy work for the auction. We'll get some help cleaning the attic, too. I want to decorate for Christmas myself, though. I can do that, can't I?"

"Only you know how you feel, and I think you 'feel' pretty good!" Tim stated as he nuzzled her neck and rubbed her shoulders.

"There's just one problem, Tim. There's no money left. It's going to take some cash to put on this shindig. I've already spent everything I have on the house. Sarah thinks you have, too. She says that you paid the contractors with your own money."

"Well, I've got some CDs and some bonds left, or I could call my father and…"

"No, don't do that!" Jake interrupted as he came into the room. "I overheard your conversation about the money. I'll pawn my mother's ruby and diamond brooch. It's worth thousands. Then, after the auction, I'll pay it off. It was going to be yours anyway, Jenna. Now it can help make your dream come true. I just hate that you two have had to spend so much of your own money. I know you've been protecting me. We haven't discussed this, but I've already arranged for you two to inherit the Inn someday. You've put your heart and souls into this place. You've done so much for me, this can be my way of thanking you."

Jenna and Tim tried to talk him out of pawning the brooch, but he wouldn't take 'no' for an answer. It was a matter of pride and they respected his decision.

Chapter 18

The next morning arrived cool and crisp. Janna woke to the sound of a car in the driveway. *It's probably Roberto*, she thought as she turned over and went back to sleep. The warm, mouthwatering scents of turkey and pumpkin pie drifted up the stairway as Jenna came down to get her morning coffee.

"Happy Thanksgiving, Jen!" Tim announced as she walked into the kitchen, yawning.

A lady grabbed her from behind and gave her a big hug. "I'm so glad to finally meet you, Jenna. Jim, come over here and meet Jenna!"

Oh Lord, Jenna thought. *My hair is a mess*. She had on Tim's robe and her old fuzzy slippers. "This isn't exactly the way I wanted to look when I met you for the first time, but I'm sure glad you came," Jenna announced as she adjusted the robe and combed through her hair with her fingers.

"You look beautiful to us," Tim's father said as he kissed her on the cheek.

She flashed that beautiful winning smile that Tim loved so much and Jim and Lisa McConnell were hooked. They loved her immediately. Not only because she made them feel welcome, but because she made their son so happy. Tim had become a different person and they knew that Jenna was the reason.

119

Roberto was preparing Thanksgiving dinner and one sidelong look at Jenna told her that he wanted all these people out of his kitchen. He was chopping vegetables with a vengeance.

"Tim, why don't you and Jake take your parents for a tour of the house while I get presentable? I'll meet you in the solarium for coffee in a bit." Jenna excused herself and went to get dressed.

They seem nice, she thought as she went up the stairs. *Not at all the 'high society' type.* She hurriedly showered and dressed. Jenna wanted Tim's parents to have the suite when they came, so she rushed around changing the bedding, dusting, and taking her clothes and belongings to another bedroom.

Jenna hadn't done anything but lie around for a week and now, she suddenly felt hot and a little dizzy as she sat down next to Tim in the solarium. "The house is beautiful, Jenna. You've done a wonderful job," Lisa said, appreciating all the hard labor that had been done. "Tim told us how much work there's been. No wonder it wore you down. How are you feeling now, dear? We've been so concerned."

"I'm getting better each day, thank you."

"Tim tells us you're planning a Governor's Ball for the new opening. It sounds so exciting."

Jenna and Lisa chatted like old friends as Tim helped his father get acquainted with Jake. The two men had never met, but they got along from the first moment. Jim was interested in the history of the old house and his ancestors. That was all it took to become Jake's pal.

Roberto and Teddy joined the little family in the dining room for dinner. Jake attempted to carve the turkey, but Tim had to finish it. Jenna said grace, "Heavenly Father, thank you for our dear friends and family. We know Annie is with us here today, happy that we are all together. We are thankful for this delicious food and for this house that has brought us all together at last. Amen."

They sat, leisurely enjoying the delicious meal of turkey and dressing with all the trimmings. Everyone praised Roberto for the fine fare. Jake shared his stories of past holidays and Jenna told how much she missed having a family on days like this. "Thanksgiving and Christmas are the hardest for me. They're such family times. It's so nice to be able to share this day with all of you."

"Well, you'll be part of our family soon. Won't she, Tim?" Lisa asked as she turned to her son.

Tim's face turned beet red and he stammered something about being too busy to worry about a wedding. He hurriedly changed the subject. "Dad, did I tell you we want to serve our own beef when the Inn opens? Jen thought of it. Roberto has some great meals planned, most featuring the McConnell beef. Teddy and I are talking about increasing the herd. What do you think?"

"I don't know one end of a cow from the other, but it sounds good to me," his father laughed. "Your grandfather would be so proud of you son, proud of you all," he added as he looked across the table at Jake, who beamed with new found pride.

Tim was relieved that the estate looked so good before his parents came. He had told them how rundown things had become, but was glad that they hadn't seen it that way. Now it would always be beautiful in their memories; just as it had been for his grandfather.

They sat in the parlor having their pie and coffee in front of the fire. "We probably shouldn't have come, but we wanted to know that you were going to be alright, Jenna," Lisa remarked as she folded her napkin and placed it near her cup and saucer. "Tim sounded so worried when he called, we thought maybe we could come and help somehow."

Tim could feel Jenna's mind whirling. "Well, if you really mean that, I know exactly how you can help," Jenna announced. "We need to sort and pack in the attic before Monday. How about helping us with that?"

Tim was mortified at the suggestion and gave Jenna a quick unapproving glare. Just then his father stood up and said, "We'd love to!"

Up to the attic they tromped, Jenna leading the way. They spent the afternoon laughing, sorting and trying on old hats. Tim's parents were enjoying every minute of it. Jake supervised by saying, "keep it" or "pack it" to every item they held up.

Tim had already suggested that his parents come for the Ball and stay for Christmas. So, when Jenna came across some old gowns, she and Lisa decided that they should wear them to the festivities. Lisa chose a long antique gown of ivory lace. Jenna found a short black beaded gown from the twenties. "Do I look like a flapper?" she asked as they modeled the beautiful dresses for the men.

Jenna was having fun today, too. It made packing the attic easier on everyone, especially Jake. He reminisced all afternoon. Jim and Lisa were a willing new audience.

It was well after 8 p.m. when they came down for cold turkey sandwiches and salad. Roberto had gone home shortly after dinner to be with his family, so Jenna and Lisa worked in the kitchen. It seemed they'd become friends.

The next three days were spent getting to know each other; eating, visiting, finishing the attic, taking quiet walks together in the woods. They reminisced about Tim's childhood, laughed, cried and had an old-fashioned family style holiday weekend. Tim continually made sure that Jenna rested.

On Saturday, Teddy hitched up the horses and took them on a hayride across the creek and over to Doc Thompson's stables. Jim and Lisa sang, "Over the River and Through the Woods" all the way home. Jenna looked across the wagon at Tim. He smiled at her and shook his head, pretending that his parents were embarrassing him. But, Jenna knew he was thrilled that they were having such a good time. As the wagon rumbled along in the brisk fall air, Jim and Lisa seemed right at home, surrounded by the land their ancestors had loved so much.

On Sunday, their suitcases sat near the front door. "Jenna, we are so glad you're feeling better. You've done such a great job with the house. Now just don't overdo getting ready for the Ball," Lisa insisted as she embraced Jenna one last time.

"I won't. Tim will see to that. We're so glad you came. It was wonderful to meet both of you."

Tim helped them out with their luggage and they all said their goodbyes. Jake waved from the doorway as the car drove down the drive. The late autumn leaves crunched underfoot as Tim and Jenna walked back to the house arm in arm. It had been a great weekend. The warmth of family had been a tonic to their weary souls.

The movers arrived early the next morning and carefully removed the antiques from the attic and carriage house that had been tagged and catalogued for the auction. Three large vans were packed to the brim with furniture and boxes, each carefully covered with packing blankets. This was valuable cargo and the movers knew it. Jake watched from the verandah as Tim and Jenna shook hands with the last driver and waved farewell.

It was late afternoon as the convoy of trucks left the house. Tears rolled down Jake's weathered old cheeks and onto his shirt. He watched the movers round the bend and disappear down the road. A lifetime of collections and memories were packed away in heavy gray blankets heading toward other lives to make new memories for new people. Jake only hoped they would appreciate the beauty of those precious antiques, even half as much as he had.

Jenna put her arm around him and guided him back to the house. She gently led him into the den and helped him sit back into the large leather chair behind the desk. She gave him a kiss on the cheek and quietly left him alone with his memories. The den had become his favorite room, for it still held the most links to his past. He sat there wishing Annie would walk in and comfort him just once more.

Chapter 19

Jake grieved over the antiques the next few days, but his period of mourning was short-lived. He now stood, pointing out the different features on the mural to a room full of reporters. Jenna's news conference was in full swing. Photographers from all across Missouri were in attendance, taking pictures and asking questions. Cameras flashed and TV crews dragged cables from one room to another.

Jake was back in his glory, explaining the history of the Governor's Ball, rattling off names and dates with pinpoint accuracy. The neighbor ladies Jenna had hired, worked for two days dusting and polishing the mirrors, crystal, brass and silver. The Inn sparkled from every camera angle.

Roberto served a gourmet lunch in the solarium and the news crews took a collective sigh when he wheeled in a cart of pastries, pies and rich desserts. They descended on him, each hoping for their favorite treat. He beamed with pride as they scrambled for the chocolate chiffon pies and mile-high cream puffs.

His creations received rave reviews in that evening's edition, across the state. One TV reporter couldn't stop commenting on the delicious food served at the Inn at Willow Creek. Another said, "This beautiful Inn will prove to be the perfect setting for the 'Governor's Ball'". Jenna flipped through the channels, seeing the house from a new prospective. It looked wonderful on television. Now, if only the rest of the world would think so.

The phone started ringing before the newscast was over and rang constantly for the next week. "We're booked solid for the holidays!" Jenna announced. "There have been people calling all day. Every weekend through January and February are booked also. Oh, and guess what? The Public Television crew wants to do a documentary on the Ball and its history. They're coming down tomorrow to talk to us. Isn't that great?" She was beaming.

"See Jen, all your hard work is finally paying off," Tim said from his ladder, as he helped the electrician with the wiring in the attic ceiling. The contractors were back, refinishing the old dance floor, insulating and paneling the cathedral ceilings. Tim insisted on recessed lighting and lots of plug-ins behind the small stage in the corner. Jenna had picked out bar stools, tables and chairs to match the beautiful old twenty-foot oak bar that stood along one wall. It had a brass foot rail and black padded armrests.

The construction and furniture bills would be paid after the auction, but Jake had to pawn the beautiful brooch in order to stock the bar and pay for the groceries Roberto would need in the coming days.

Jenna sent out 100 engraved invitations. Politicians, businessmen and community leaders from across the state were coming for the event. Tim had hired a small dance band from St. Louis, who played everything from blues to disco and Jenna planned to decorate everything for Christmas. It would be gorgeous; at least that was the plan. After all, a lot was riding on the big night.

Jenna had saved as many of the antique decorations as she could salvage; blown glass ornaments from Germany in every size and color. Now, she scoured the countryside and every discount store in the county for gold and ivory Christmas balls, lights and ornaments. She bought yards of gold ribbons and had the nursery deliver several trees and what seemed like a mile of evergreen garland.

The weekend before the Ball, Tim, Jenna and all the help started decorating. A 10-foot poinsettia tree was constructed in the solarium. The garland was draped everywhere, even down three stories on both sides of the huge staircase. Bead studded velvet strawberries filled a crystal bowl in the entry. Gold gilded flying angels were placed on both sides of the mirror above the fireplace in the parlor. Sarah had come to help and smiled to see such a glorious sight. Tim put mistletoe in the doorways and caught Jenna for a kiss every time she went through.

"Will you two stop that?" Sarah laughed, as she set candles along the garland, down the center of the dining room table. "We've got work to do." She could see how happy Jenna and Tim seemed. Maybe their dreams would finally come true. Sarah still fretted about their money situation. She had become the designated worrier.

* * *

The morning of December 18th, dawned gray and threatening. Snow was blowing into small drifts along the driveway, as Tim drove out and down the road. He was headed for St. Louis and the auction. The early morning newscast cautioned drivers that traffic was moving slowly on the interstate and to take special care. They were forecasting snow and ice for the next few days. Tim didn't know when he'd get back.

"Just be careful," Jenna had insisted as she kissed him goodbye.

"I'll call you tonight. I love you."

"I love you more," Jenna stated as she closed the door against the brisk wind. She had watched out the frosty window as his car disappeared down the road. She and Jake had planned to go too, but Jake broke down at the dinner table the day before. "I can't go. Don't be mad, but I just can't go." Jake blotted his eyes with a napkin.

"We're not mad," Jenna had said gently, "we understand completely. But, if you don't care, I'd like to stay here with you tomorrow. Tim can go and give us a full report."

Tim had nodded in agreement. He knew the auction would have been very emotional for Jake. It would be better for him to stay home with Jenna. Tim's parents were flying to St. Louis for the auction and would drive back with him for the Ball.

The house seemed quiet now with Tim gone and Jenna was a little at loose ends. She drifted from one room to another, putting the finishing touches on the decorations.

She braced herself against the wind to get to the summer kitchen. There was one smaller tree to put up and she decided to spend the day working on it with Jake. As she pulled the door shut behind her, carefully hanging onto the little tree, a small drift above the door let go and snow fell down the back of her neck. She shivered and hurried to the kitchen door, stomping her snowy feet and taking off her boots.

Roberto was taking a sheet of cookies from the oven as she came in, tree in hand. Jake sat near the fire with his coffee, sadly looking into the flickering flames. "Let's not let this be a sad day. I want you boys to help me with this tree. It's the last one. It's for your room, Jake," Jenna announced as she put the tree into its metal stand.

"I don't need any dumb Christmas tree!" he barked.

"Sure you do," Jenna insisted. "Even Teddy has his own tree. I helped him finish it last night."

"There's a tree in every room already. I go to the bathroom just to get away from all the decorations."

"Oh, don't be such an old humbug. This will be a very special Christmas. We'll get to share this wonderful home with lots of people again. This tree, however, will be yours and yours alone."

She popped popcorn and brought a bowl of cranberries from the cooler. She turned the radio to a station playing Christmas carols and sat down beside Jake near the fire. "Come on Roberto. Sit down and grab a needle!"

After lots of grumbling, Roberto finally sat down and started threading popcorn and cranberries with Jake and Jenna. Before long, all three of them were humming along with the music. They all joined in to sing, "It's beginning to look a lot like Christmas!" Hundred of cranberries later, they wound the garland on Jake's little tree and plugged in the lights. They placed the tree close to Jake's chair next to the window in his room.

Jenna had saved a box of old glass ornaments that Annie had used years ago. She brought them in to Jake and reminisced about each shiny Santa and toy as they hung each on their own special branch. In the bottom of the box was a paper snowflake with the message, "Merry Christmas! Love, Jenna (age 8)".

"Annie always loved this snowflake, Jenna."

"I know," she said as she brushed away a tear. Jake put the delicate snowflake in a place of honor as they walked out into the warm kitchen, leaving the little tree twinkling against the snowy window. They spent the rest of the afternoon helping Roberto decorate Christmas cookies, eating all their mistakes, laughing and singing along with the radio.

That evening, the phone rang just as they were sitting down to dinner. It was Tim. "How was your trip?" Jenna asked.

"Okay. Slow, but okay. Mom and dad's plane was delayed and we were an hour late getting to the auction. Everything is going good. Some things are going for less than the appraisal, but most are going a lot higher. The auctioneers expect it will last until at least ten o'clock tonight. They'll finish then tomorrow. We'll try to come home sometime on Wednesday, if the weather doesn't get worse."

"It's still snowing here, too," Jenna announced as she pulled the curtain back and looked at the lights in Teddy's loft. She could barely see them as the heavy snow whirled around the carriage house. "I miss you, Tim."

"I miss you, too. How was Jake today? I couldn't stop thinking of him as the sale went on."

"We had a wonderful day. Jake and Roberto helped me decorate the last tree and we made cookies. We even sang a few carols," Jenna said as she smiled at Jake across the table.

"Jenna, you are really something. Only you could turn this into a good day for him. Tell him everyone here is commenting on how beautiful the antiques are. I wish you were here, but I know he needs you. Dad's motioning for me to hurry up. I've got to get back. See you on Wednesday."

"Okay, bye!"

"Oh, and Jen..."

"Yes"

"I love you."

"I love you, too; very much. Goodnight."

Jenna told Jake that everyone was enchanted by the antiques and the sale was going well. He smiled a sad smile and Jenna changed the subject to the weather.

The next morning the snow had stopped but the wind still howled from the north. Jenna helped Roberto in the kitchen all morning, then finished decorating the attic.

She covered every table with white tablecloths that she had rented from a linen service in Blakesburg. It's the same service that would bring clean linens and sheets to the Inn twice a week after they opened.

She placed evergreen and candles in the center of each table and set place cards at each chair around the room.

Jenna checked the list of guests over and over. Seating the correct people together was going to prove interesting, to say the least. She had called the governor's office several times that week, trying to get the seating chart just right.

"If you seat Senator Ross next to Senator Stevens, you might be sorry," the secretary warned. "They could kill each other." Jenna laughed, but the secretary saw no humor in the situation. Jenna was getting nervous now. *What have I gotten myself into?*

The contractors put one last coat of wax on the dance floor and tried to get back to town before the roads drifted shut again.

She was finally ready for the Ball and the opening. The guests would start arriving early Saturday morning. She walked from room to room checking out every detail. What was she forgetting? After all the months of hard work, she couldn't believe that the house was finally ready.

Time seemed to stand still as Jenna waited for Tim and his parents to return from St. Louis. The haunting feeling that she was forgetting something bothered her all morning Wednesday, as she paced back and forth in the entryway; checking and rechecking her ever-present lists.

It was mid-afternoon when they finally arrived. Tim carried in the luggage as Jim and Lisa hurried to the house with arm loads of packages in bright paper and ribbons. The sight of them carrying Christmas gifts suddenly hit Jenna like a ton of bricks. Now she knew what she had forgotten: Christmas presents! She hadn't had time to think about Christmas shopping. Now, she would only have two days to do it all. She made a quick mental list: Jake, Tim, Teddy, Roberto, Jim and Lisa. Oh yes, and Sarah. What could she get them at this late date?

"Welcome home!" Jenna smiled as she opened the door.

Tim and his parents had lots of news and couldn't wait to tell Jake and Jenna about the auction. Representatives from museums and historical societies had come to bid on the antiques as well as the general public. The news that it was a sale from the "Inn at Willow Creek", the home of the next Governor's Ball, had brought in more people than expected. The new notoriety had greatly increased the values.

With the IRS and auction fees paid, Tim and Jenna reimbursed, the bank mortgage, insurance, taxes and contractors paid, it looked as if there would be about $85,000 left. That would give them some working capital to get through the first year. After that, hopefully it would pay for itself.

It was a huge weight being lifted from their shoulders. Jenna and Tim hugged. She could feel the tension leave her body, as she relaxed in his arms. "It's going to happen. It's really going to happen!" She sighed.

The next few days were a flurry of activity. Jenna took Lisa Christmas shopping. They worked on the attic, helped make canapés and appetizers, had their hair and nails done and wrapped the presents. They even stopped to have lunch together in town. They were busy, but the financial stress was over and Jenna was finally enjoying the frenzy and excitement of Christmas.

The Governor's Ball was a very special night. Jake, Tim and his father stood together in the entry hall, patiently waiting for Jenna and Lisa. The men looked handsome and sophisticated in their black tuxedos. Lisa finally appeared in her beautiful lace gown. She waited with the men, straightening their ties and brushing their shoulders.

They all looked up. There she was at the top of the stairs. Jenna took Tim's breath away. She was wearing the black beaded gown and she glided down the stairway like a queen. Her hair was piled high on her head and her dark eyes glistened in the twinkling Christmas lights along the stairs. "You're beautiful!" Tim exclaimed as he met her on the last step. He handed her a tiny gold box. Inside, she found the ruby and diamond brooch.

"I retrieved it from the pawn shop today. Jake wants you to have it. It's only appropriate that you wear it tonight."

She threw her arms around Tim and kissed him, then turned to Jake and kissed him, too. "I can't begin to tell you what this means to me," Jenna said, as tears welled up in her eyes.

It was snowing lightly and the Inn looked like a beautiful Christmas card as the guests arrived in limousines and fancy cars. Jake, Tim and Jenna greeted everyone at the door. "Merry Christmas, Senator Morton. Welcome, Governor Ellington." Jake was in fine form.

The press photographers were everywhere, snapping pictures of the governors and their wives, the senators and VIPs. The election in November had been heated, but tonight that was all behind them, as they danced the night away. The evening seemed to be a success.

Tim and Jenna mingled with the rich and famous, while Jim and Lisa seemed right at home with the politicians and businessmen. Jake told stories about the other Balls and tales of "moonshine" and holidays past. There was music and laughter everywhere. Roberto saw to it that food and drink was plentiful and delicious. He dictated every move the hired waiters made. Teddy helped out behind the bar and Sarah guided guests to the powder room or took their coats. The evening moved on like a well-oiled machine.

Each governor made a short speech and toasted their hosts, the McConnells and the Inn at Willow Creek. In reply, Jake gave a toast to the old and new administrations and to a prosperous four years ahead for the great state of Missouri. That statement received a standing ovation from the guests and reporters. Then, Jake introduced Tim and Jenna to the crowd.

Tim took the microphone. "On behalf of my family, I'd like to thank all of you for coming tonight and for making the opening of the Inn such a special occasion. The Governor's Ball is a great old tradition and we hope it will continue. I must give credit where credit is due, however. This beautiful Inn and wonderful evening were all the vision of this lovely lady, Miss Jenna Adams." Tim held out his hand to her. "I'm hoping to persuade her to become Mrs. Timothy McConnell next June."

Cameras flashed, everyone stood up and applauded. Jenna bowed and stepped forward, a little overwhelmed by all the attention. The band played, "I'll be home for Christmas," and the governors danced the last dance with their wives. They motioned for Tim and Jenna to join them.

"Did you just announce that we are getting married in June?" Jenna asked as they stepped onto the dance floor.

"You bet I did! Setting a date is my Christmas gift to you. I only did it because I haven't had time to find a real gift," Tim teased as they glided around the floor. They'd never danced before, it felt right.

She kissed his neck, closed her eyes and followed his lead. The other guests poured onto the floor as Tim held her close. This was a magical time to remember, their first Christmas together.

Chapter 20

The weeks and months following Christmas had gone very well for the Inn. They'd stayed busy, about 75% filled. Not bad for the winter months. They had sleigh rides in the snow, two more dances, some Sunday morning brunches and lots of activities. They were even making plans for the first horse show in April.

Roberto had made quite a name for himself at the Ball, serving his beautiful appetizers and desserts. People were calling now, making reservations for his meals and special creations. They had four weddings and several anniversary weekends reserved for the summer, but they held the week of June 12th open for their own wedding.

The plans were taking over Jenna's life and Tim just stayed out of the way. There wasn't much for him to do. He was working in the rooms on the north side of the house that there hadn't been enough time or money to finish before the opening. Jake was giving his mini tours each day and loving every minute of it. They'd all slipped into the quiet routine of the Inn. It wasn't a hustle and bustle lifestyle. It was slow and relaxed.

When guests didn't feel like joining the rest in the dining room for breakfast, Jenna took them a large basket filled with carafes of coffee or orange juice, added fresh fruit, muffins and pastries from the oven. She wrapped antique silverware in the beautiful cloth napkins, put in small china plates with matching cups and saucers. She'd place the fragrant basket of goodies outside their door, knock and hurry away. It was as if it arrived out of nowhere.

People were there to relax and the slower pace was good for everyone. Or was it? Jenna was content running the Inn, greeting guests, taking care of Jake and loving Tim. They were staying at her apartment when the Inn was full.

One night, Jenna awoke to find Tim looking out the window. He seemed so restless and distant lately; quieter than usual.

"What's wrong, Tim?" Jenna asked through the darkness.

"Nothing's wrong."

"You seem so unhappy. Is it me? Have I done something wrong?"

"No, of course not," he said as he came over to the bed and sat down beside her. "You do such a great job with the guests, with the business, with everything. You don't need me around. I'm beginning to feel like a glorified bellhop."

Jenna could feel a sudden knot in her stomach. She hadn't seen it coming. *He wants out; he wants to get back to the city; back to more excitement. It has been fun fixing up the Inn, but now he must be bored with the day to day routine.* She felt ill. What was happening? "Tim, I need you. The Inn needs you. You're no bellhop! I couldn't do it without you."

"I know. It's no big deal. Go back to sleep, I'm just thinking. Don't worry about it, really. Just go back to sleep." Tim went out to the kitchen.

How was she supposed to go back to sleep? She tossed and turned all night. Her stomach churned. She tried to think why Tim seemed so down. Had she treated him like a bellhop? He did carry the guests' luggage sometimes and once someone did try to tip him. She had laughed, but he didn't think it was funny. *Tomorrow I'll try to hire someone to take care of luggage and that sort of thing. I'll include Tim in more of the business decisions. I'll change. I'll do whatever it takes to make him happy.*

Her alarm went off at 5:30 a.m., as usual. Jenna sat straight up. She heard Tim's car backing out of her driveway. She dressed quickly and hurried over to the Inn, but his car wasn't there.

Roberto was taking apple turnovers out of the oven. "Where's Tim? The faucet is leaking in the main bathroom," Roberto remarked as she rushed past.

"Get someone from town to fix it, Tim's busy!" Jenna barked as she headed down the hall to the den. Normally she would sit down with Roberto over coffee and plan the next day's menu. She closed the door and sat down behind the desk. Tears came. *What have I done? Where could he have gone so early in the morning? Are we hurrying too fast? Maybe he feels trapped. We don't have to get married in June, we could wait awhile. That must be it!* She had to find him and tell him they'd postpone the wedding. *No big deal, I'm scared too. That's only natural.*

She ran past Roberto, who decided now wasn't a good time to ask for a raise and headed her car towards Blakesburg. *Maybe he is at his office in town.* No, no one was at the office. *It's only 6:30 a.m. for heaven's sake, he wouldn't meet a client at this hour.*

She headed back toward the Inn. There at the edge of town was Tim's car sitting next to a little red BMW in the parking lot of the roadhouse. Jenna didn't pull in. She drove slowly back to the Inn, back to the business at hand. She'd pretend that nothing was wrong.

Tim showed up a little before nine. "Sorry I'm late, Jen. I had some business to take care of."

"You're not late. You don't have to punch a time clock."

"Sorry about last night, Jen. ·I couldn't sleep. I just needed to sort some things out."

"Did you get them all sorted?" Jenna asked cautiously.

"Well, kind of. I've decided to go to Chicago and see my folks. I need to talk to them. You know, get their opinion on some things. You can get along without me for a few days, can't you?"

"Sure, we're not too busy right now. Take as long as you need." Jenna couldn't look him in the eye. She was afraid looking into them might tell her more than she wanted to know. "When are you leaving?"

"The sooner the better; I may go this afternoon."

She avoided him all morning busying herself with things at the opposite end of the house. She was trying not to let him know how much she was hurting. At noon he tracked her down. She'd been sorting linens upstairs.

"I'm all packed. Aren't you going to tell me goodbye?" Tim asked as he walked as fast as he could to keep up with her in the hall.

"Sure, goodbye. Tell your folks, hello for me." She gave him a peck on the cheek.

"Are you mad that I'm not taking you with me?"

"No, not at all. You'd better get going so it doesn't get too late. I'm fine," Jenna insisted.

"I'll call you in a day or so." He picked up his suitcase and headed for the door. "I love you, Jen."

"I love you more."

* * *

The next few days were excruciating for Jenna. She found it almost impossible to smile at the guests. Roberto was driving her crazy with little things that were unimportant. Even Jake was getting on her nerves. The fun of running the Inn just wasn't the same with Tim gone.

She hired a maintenance man named Benny Robertson, who had answered an ad for bellhop/maintenance worker. His job description included: lawn mower, plumber, electrician, baggage handler, dishwasher, mechanic, etc. Maybe she <u>had</u> expected Tim to do all the dirty work. No wonder he was sick of it.

He called from Chicago, but never really said when he'd be back. She tried to get him to tell her what day he'd return. "Doc Thompson wants to meet with us on Monday. We have to finalize the plans for the horse show," Jenna hesitated, thinking he'd say something. "And, don't forget the "wild bunch" are coming the next weekend on 'Spring Break', you know for the weekend you promised them.

All Tim said was, "Oh, that's right." No hint of when he'd be home. He was coming home, wasn't he?

"Have you seen Ellen since you were back?"

"As a matter of fact, we had lunch today," Tim answered nonchalantly.

Jenna quickly changed the subject. "I hired a guy to mow the lawn, carry the luggage, that sort of thing. I hope that's all right?"

"You're the boss!"

"I don't want you to feel like a bellhop."

"Jenna, that was just an expression. Don't worry about it. Here, Mom wants to talk to you. I'll call again later. Bye."

Jenna never heard a word his mother said to her. She was devastated. Tim never said he missed her or that he loved her. He was being evasive and secretive again. He'd even had lunch with Ellen. What did that mean? Were they just old friends meeting for lunch or was there more to it?

The weekend seemed endless. Jenna felt as though everything was in slow motion. She hadn't slept and nothing sounded good to eat. She sat alone in her apartment trying to think of what she would say if Tim were to walk in.

"I know what's going on, don't try to deny it" or "Tim, I love you. I'll do anything to make you stay." She wasn't sure how she'd react.

He called several times, acting as if he wanted to tell her something, then holding back, not really saying anything. He asked about the Inn or about Jake, but never anything about Jenna or what he was doing. He was keeping something from her and he didn't know how to tell her.

*   *   *

Monday morning errands took Jenna to Blakesburg. There in front of the real estate office stood Tim, leaning against the little red BMW, talking to whoever was inside. All that Jenna could see was someone with short, blonde hair. *How could he? He's back, but didn't come out to the Inn first. He had to get to town. How could he?*

She speeded up, not wanting him to see her. She did her errands and returned to the Inn, but Tim was still not back. Now she knew how she'd react when she saw him, Jenna was furious. She slammed the packages onto the kitchen counter.

"Roberto, if Tim stops by, tell him I've gone to meet with Doc Thompson! We're supposed to meet him at his house, not at the stables." She hurried off to the meeting, so hurt and angry she was shaking.

Not long after she left, Tim finally arrived, tired from driving all night. He'd forgotten they were to meet with Doc Thompson. The new maintenance man was carrying trash out the back door.

"Who are you" Tim asked, "and where's Jenna?"

"I'm Benny Robertson. I'm not sure where Jenna went, but I heard her tell Roberto that she was going to some doctor's house."

"Doc Thompson's stables?"

"No, she definitely said house, not the stables. I'm new here, so I don't know for sure."

She's at some doctor's house. Now, Tim was angry. *I've only been gone a few days and she is seeing Chuck Davis again, at his house no less. I called her almost every day from Chicago and she never said anything. I knew she was upset about something.* He thought it was because he hadn't taken her along to see his parents. He'd come back with so much news to tell her, and now she was with Chuck.

Tim stomped around outside for 20 minutes, showing Benny where all the water shutoffs were and how to turn the electricity on to the guest cottage. From the corner of his eye, he saw Jenna getting out of the car. He left poor Benny in the middle of a sentence and rushed over to meet her.

"I'm only gone for four days and you sneak off to meet Chuck again. At his house no less!"

"What are you talking about?"

"The new guy said you went to meet the doctor at his house."

"I met Doc Thompson at his house. Where were you, we were both supposed to be there. What's all this about Chuck?"

Tim felt stupid. "Oh, Jenna, I'm sorry honey! I forgot about the meeting with Doc. When that Benny guy said you were at the doctor's house, I thought he meant Chuck. I just saw red. I flew off the handle; I'm sorry." Tim said as he tried to embrace her.

She pushed him away. He had set her off again. "Listen, mister, if anyone should be upset here, it's me!" She moved past him and into the house. The guests were looking at them and whispering. She didn't want to make a scene.

Tim followed her down the hall to the den and shut the door. "Why are you upset? I asked you if it was okay to leave for a few days. You seemed fine with it."

"Tim, I know something's going on with you; something you haven't told me about. I've seen you with that blonde in the BMW, twice! I know you're not happy here anymore. If you don't love me, just tell me. Don't go behind my back. Is it Ellen or that blonde? I know it's not very exciting for you out here in the country. I know I've treated you like the hired help. I'm sorry for that and I can change those things. But, I can't make you love me."

"Oh, Jen, you've totally misunderstood everything. I'm so sorry. I should have never made that crack about feeling like a bellhop. I love this old house. I plan to be here forever. What I was trying to say that night was that you don't need me all the time anymore. I've been working on a deal to buy some property from Bill Harris, the blonde in the BMW. I wanted to surprise you. I've decided to start my own real estate agency again. I went to Chicago to see what my father thought of the idea. I met with Ellen, to have her look over the contracts for the new office complex that we'll put on the Harris property." Tim held her. "We, you and me. Your name will be on that contract, too. Unless you think it's a terrible idea?"

"Tim, why didn't you tell me? I thought I was losing you. I've been terrified. I knew you were distracted, keeping something from me. I thought you were bored with me and having an affair."

"Whoa! Where did you get the idea that I was bored? Being with you is anything but boring! And, as for an affair, you're all I'll ever want or need. I love you! Don't you know that by now?" He kissed her longingly, needing to show her how much he cared.

Relief finally swept over her and she relaxed. "Tim, if you want to start your own business, I'm behind you 100%. I know you love real estate."

"Oh, thank God!" he exclaimed. "I thought you'd be upset with me. I've been afraid you wouldn't understand my need to make a living on my own, to support our kids, to be my own boss. I can set my own hours and I'll still help out around here, I promise. But the Inn is your project now, yours and Jake's."

"Did you say, kids?" Jenna asked with a smile. "Our kids?"

They held each other, finally secure in their love for one another; knowing that neither of them was ever going to leave; knowing that their family would make the Inn a success and still be able to have a life of their own.

*   *   *

Spring Break week was held open for the "no-work" vacation Tim had promised. The gang came on a Saturday and stayed the whole next week.

Roberto had been instructed to feed them anything they wanted, so he did. He wasn't proud of it, but he did it. Their meals consisted of chili dogs and burritos, pizza and beer, nachos and cheese with ketchup on everything. He grumbled a lot, for it was not his usual gourmet menu. Everyone loved it; except for the other guests at the Inn. The "wild bunch" took over and Jenna spent the whole week trying to explain their actions. "I'm sorry the peanut fight in the gazebo got so out of hand. They're just kids, I'm sorry. I'm sorry the volleyball hit your car, Mr. Taylor. They'll only be here for a few more days. Yes, Mrs. Oliver, those are rubber chickens on the grill; but you'll get the real ones tonight."

During their stay, Tim and Jenna asked the gang to stand up with them at their wedding. They were thrilled. It would be held in the gazebo in the garden; the beautiful garden that they had all helped to create. Jake would give Jenna away and after the wedding, Teddy would give them a ride around the grounds in the old carriage. After the reception, Tim would carry Jenna off to their little honeymoon cottage in the woods. Then they'd spend a week at the Lake of the Ozarks.

Keri and Samantha went wild. They plotted and planned with Jenna all week. They went to town and picked out dresses and decided on heather and wildflowers for their hair. Jenna ordered invitations. She had an entire notebook filled with lists; guests, food, music, clothes, honeymoon, flowers, and thank-you's. Keri drew sketches of what the cake should look like. Samantha decided the color of the punch and the type of sandwiches. They hired a lady to play the harp in the garden and gave instructions to Roberto about every tiny detail. Jenna just shook her head and laughed. She knew that he would do things his way. He always did. But, it would be perfect, she was sure of that. "I'll be fine if I don't lose my lists," she stated.

Meanwhile the boys went fishing, drank beer, rode horses, played cards and watched basketball on TV. "Guy stuff" as Tim called it. One afternoon when the girls left for town, Tim showed the guys the north side of the house. He was secretly turning it into a private apartment for him and Jenna. It had an outside entrance through the summer kitchen and an indoor entrance through the pantry. It looked out into the woods. He was converting the large storage room into a kitchen and dining room area, with a big family room at one end. Tim planned to put French doors onto the patio that he would build in the summer. They would be surrounded by the woods that Jenna loved so much. It would give them a shady retreat for some time alone. All this time, Jenna thought he was making an extra suite for the Inn. The boys were sworn to secrecy. "Don't even tell Keri or Mouse," Tim demanded.

The old sitting room would eventually be their bedroom and bath. Tim had even drawn up plans to make the summer kitchen into rooms for their children someday. Jenna was so busy with the Inn and the wedding plans, that she had no idea that he was restoring it for her and their own little family. It would be a great wedding surprise.

The Inn was a reality now and the "wild bunch" had helped make it happen. Their friendship had helped get them through the toughest times. Their hard work and encouragement had made it the showplace it had been so many years before. Their laughter brought joy back to the old house, joy it had longed for all those years.

This little band had been a "God send" to everyone. They had always made Jake feel special. They took time to listen to his tales. They had helped encourage Teddy, always including him in their projects and decisions. They also knew how to make Tim laugh and helped bring Jenna's dream to life.

The last morning of their visit as they prepared to leave, Samantha handed Tim and Jenna a thank-you gift in appreciation for their "Spring Break". It was wrapped and tied with a big red bow. Jenna couldn't wait to open it. Inside was a large mailbox that read, "THE INN AT WILLOW CREEK." She cried and kissed them all.

Suddenly, Tim remembered the old rusty mailbox down the road that read, "J.J. McConnell." It had been exactly one year ago that he saw it, saw the house and saw his darling Jenna for the very first time.

Chapter 21

The tall, old oak trees above stippled the patio with sunshine and shade as Jenna sat cross-legged in the big, macramé hammock. "Tim, are you listening to me?"

"No, I'm not. Any great chef can tell you that it is impossible to concentrate on business while creating a masterpiece," Tim answered as he stood barefoot behind the gas grill, spatula in hand.

"I hardly think hamburgers would be considered a masterpiece."

"That, my dear, depends on who you ask?"

"Tim, would you be serious for just a minute? I never seem to get you to myself anymore. We really need to talk. Come sit with me." Jenna patted the hammock beside her.

"Do you remember what happened the last time we were both in that hammock?" he asked as he turned down the heat under the burgers and started toward her, grinning.

"Whoa, now," Jenna protested. "It's broad daylight."

"Well, I guess the honeymoon really is over. What do you need to talk about?"

Jenna sorted through the notes she had crammed into her ever-present clipboard, as Tim sat down beside her, nearly spilling them both onto the ground.

The June horse show is scheduled for the 5th and 6th. Roberto wants the 8th, 9th, and 10th off. The 19th is the Gordon wedding and we're booked solid from then on until after Labor Day. What do you think?"

"I think it would be nearly impossible to stand up in this thing!" Tim answered as he tried to balance himself without tipping over.

"Tim, you're not concentrating again!"

"Honey, would you stop worrying about our vacation. I've already taken care of it. We're going to the lake for our anniversary. It was supposed to be a surprise, but you keep hounding me about it, so here it is: SURPRISE! Happy Anniversary! We'll leave Friday the 11th and come back late Sunday night. Jake and Benny can handle things for a couple of days. Teddy and Roberto will be here, too. It will be fine. I've already gone through it with them, okay?" Tim announced as he put his arms around her.

She rested her head against his chest. "Thank you, honey. You just don't know how much I need to get out of here for awhile. We haven't been away together since our honeymoon and that's been nearly two years. It's time, Tim."

Tim and Jenna were living in their own apartment on the north side of the Inn. Their patio gave them privacy from the guests, but it seemed someone was always coming around to ask questions or give suggestions, interrupting their solitude.

"Yoo-hoo, Mrs. McConnell," It was Mrs. Barton from Room 5, again. "Would it be all right if I have my sister stop and join me for tea in the gazebo this afternoon? I'd rather the other guests not be around. You understand, don't you dear?"

"God, help me," Jenna said under her breath. "Of course, Mrs. Barton, I'll keep the others in the solarium," she said, showing a fake smile to the rather plump lady who'd been driving her crazy the last few days.

She waited until Mrs. Barton rounded the corner of the house. "See what I mean, I've got to get out of here!"

"Okay, okay. A few days away will be good for us both. But Jen, it's nothing to get crazy over."

"I'm sorry. I don't know what's wrong with me. It's just that everyone gets on my nerves lately."

"Maybe you should have Doc Thompson help you with the horse show. He said he'd be glad to help. You've got to learn to delegate more responsibility and not try to do everything yourself."

"You're right. I'll call Doc tomorrow." Doc Thompson knew more about horses than anyone around, but Jenna always found it hard to ask for help. She needed to be in charge of everything.

"Did you get our room on the lakeside?" she asked. "Is it the suite we were in on our honeymoon? I wonder if my swimsuit will still fit me. I should call and make sure it's the same room."

"Stop, Jenna! I've taken care of everything and you'll look great in your suit. You always look great. Let me do this for you, will you? I'm not totally incapable, you know." There she went again, always needing to be in charge of the details; making lists, organizing, etc. *Why can't she just relax and let me handle things for awhile,* Tim wondered.

She jotted down the dates for the vacation in her daily planner, penciling it in, just in case it needed to be cancelled.

"Write it in ink, will you?" Tim said sarcastically. "Permanent ink!"

She looked at him and started to cry.

Tim got up from the hammock, "I'm going to help Teddy move the cattle to the south pasture. Put my hamburger in the refrigerator. I'll get it later." Tim was tired of riding the rollercoaster that Jenna had been on lately. He felt like he was walking on eggshells every time they talked, never knowing what was going to set her off.

Jenna lay back in the hammock alone, feeling sorry for herself. Tim was busy with the real estate office. He was gone most of the day, only helping out at the Inn in the evenings and weekends, while Jenna seldom left the house except for business. Roberto usually bought the groceries in town, but lately she had taken over that duty, simply to get away if only for an hour or so.

The Inn was exactly the way she had envisioned it. Now, Tim couldn't understand her need to get away all the time. Wasn't it what she had wanted? He loved their home and couldn't wait to get there each day after work. Sometimes the guests imposed on them, but that was just part of the business. Jenna knew that when she started. At first she just accepted it, but lately it was upsetting her.

Tim went to help Teddy with the cattle whenever he wanted to get away or to avoid a conflict. Since the Inn opened two and a half years ago, Teddy had been in charge of raising the beef that was served. McConnell beef was once again famous in the area. The herd had been increased to accommodate the guests. Teddy, now in his late 70's needed more help and Tim always stepped up to volunteer. It was relaxing for him, getting outside and doing something different than dealing with clients or guests. Tim was learning as much as he could about cattle from Teddy. He knew that one day soon, Teddy would have to retire, but Tim wasn't going to be the one to mention it.

They got out of the old pickup and together dragged the heavy gate open that separated the pastures. "Maybe I'm gettin' too old fer this, Tim," Teddy said as he rubbed his lower back. "I always need ya' ta' help me anymore."

"Don't worry about that. I'm glad to do it. I needed to get away from Jen anyway. She's on a rampage again."

"What's the matter now? That ol' gal in 5 again?"

"Yeh, I wish that old bitty would find another place to stay. You know, I think she has her eye on you," Tim teased. "She keeps coming back for some reason."

Teddy's face turned red, "It's not me!"

* * *

The bell in the entry hall was ringing and Jenna hurried to greet the new guests. "Good afternoon and welcome," Jenna said as she shook hands with the new arrivals.

Mr. and Mrs. Parker were from Omaha and would be staying in the large suite all week. He was a businessman who appeared to be quite wealthy. His pretty wife appeared quiet and reserved, while he was loud and obnoxious from the start.

"I understand we'll be staying in the best room in the house. Is that correct?" Mr. Parker asked.

"We have the suite and private bath reserved for you," Jenna said, smiling that fake smile.

"I didn't ask you that. I asked if we had the best room in the house?" he snapped.

"Yes, we're sure you'll be very comfortable there. I'll have Benny get your bags and I'll take you to your room," Jenna answered, fumbling for the key. Her hands were trembling. His attitude had her somewhat rattled. She led the way up the beautiful winding staircase.

"Don't you have an elevator?" Mr. Parker asked in disgust.

"I'm sorry, but the Inn has been preserved to keep its original home-like feel. That's the difference between an inn and a hotel. If you'd rather, I'd be more than happy to find you a room at a hotel in Blakesburg," Jenna offered, her fake smile getting tighter by the minute.

Mr. Parker grumbled something about driving all this way to climb a bunch of damn stairs, but followed Jenna anyway.

Benny came along behind, trying to carry the entire set of luggage at once. He was in his early twenties and as strong as an ox, but Jenna could see that he was struggling. "Here Benny, let me help you."

"Let him get it! That's what you pay him for, isn't it? I'll tip him well enough," Mr. Parker added arrogantly.

Jenna took the two smaller bags from Benny's load and hurried up the stairs.

The beautiful suite of rooms was light and airy. Jenna opened the French doors out to the balcony above the verandah. The air smelled of lilacs and the view was breathtaking. She looked out at the pond with the weeping willows dipping their long branches gracefully down to meet the water.

"If there's anything you need, please let me know. Dinner will be served in the dining room at 7:00, if you can join us."

Mr. Parker handed Benny a ten dollar bill. "No thank-you, sir. Mrs. McConnell pays me very well. I don't accept tips," Benny said as he pulled the door shut behind him.

"Since when don't you accept tips," Jenna asked halfway down the stairs.

"I wouldn't take anything from that windbag!"

Jenna gave him a hug and a peck on the cheek. "Thanks buddy. That made my day."

Benny Robertson was always there when she needed him, always coming to her rescue. He seemed to sense when things were going badly and knew exactly what to say to defuse the situation. He'd worked at the Inn for over two years now, shoveling snow, mowing lawn, carrying luggage, busing tables, whatever Jenna needed him to do. He never missed a day of work and was never late, not even once. When Jenna married Tim and moved into their apartment at the Inn, Benny rented her old room above Sarah Martin's garage.

"What's your opinion of Benny?" Sarah had asked Jenna one day out of the blue.

"He's a good worker, never complains, always there when we need him. Why do you ask?"

"I just wondered. He doesn't talk much. He always pays his rent on time, has coffee with us once in awhile at the store, but I don't know anything about him. Do you?

"I figured you were close to him. He talks about you all the time," Jenna stated, surprised that Sarah knew so little.

"All we know is that he's from Oklahoma and apparently has no family. That's all he's shared. He doesn't seem to want to talk about his past. I've tried to set him up with a date once or twice, but he says he has a girlfriend and plans to marry her. We've never seen her."

"Well," Jenna replied, "that's more than I know. He's never mentioned anything about a girlfriend, but he told me he was from Arkansas when he applied for the job."

"Don't get me wrong, Jenna. We like the guy. It's just strange that no one knows anything about him."

"Sarah, you're a worrier. I can't imagine finding anyone better than Benny. He's such a good help. We don't know what we'd do without him."

*   *   *

Jake was giving a tour of the gardens to some of the guests and Jenna rushed out to steer them all towards the solarium, away from the gazebo and Mrs. Barton's glare.

"Folks, Jake will tell you more about the house and its history, in the solarium. Roberto, our chef, has set out tea and pastries for you there," Jenna announced.

Jake led the little group toward the house and Jenna waved at Mrs. Barton and her sister. "I'll bring out your tea in just a moment, ladies."

She hurried in the back door of the kitchen and put the tea kettle on to boil. She was putting cups and saucers on a tray, when someone came up behind her. Without looking back, she asked, "Roberto, can you hand me those pastries?"

Two arms came around and grabbed hold of the counter on each side of her. She tried to turn around. It was Mr. Parker. "Mrs. McConnell, I can hand you anything you want," he said seductively. She felt his hot breath on the back of her neck. "I'm sure this will be a very memorable stay, here at your little Inn."

Just then the kettle started to whistle and Benny walked in. "Jenna, do you need some help?"

"Yes," Jenna replied, visibly shaken. "I need you to help me take these tea items out to the gazebo."

"Excuse us, Mr. Parker. I think your <u>wife</u> is looking for you," Benny said, looking Mr. Parker directly in the eye.

159

Mr. Parker backed away from Jenna and then said smugly, "Remember my offer, Mrs. McConnell, anything you want." He walked out of the room and Jenna nearly collapsed into Benny's arms.

"Are you all right? Did he hurt you?"

"I'm fine. He didn't even touch me, but it was the way he talked to me, the way he said it. Oh God, I'm glad you walked in when you did. Please, don't say anything about this to Tim, okay? He'd get crazy. I'm sure nothing like this will happen again. Mr. Parker knows you saw him. It won't happen again," she said trying to convince herself.

Chapter 22

All that week she tried to avoid Mr. Parker. In front of other people he was rude to Jenna, always complaining about the room or the service. But, when he could find her alone, he'd flirt with her; wooing her, standing close to her. Too close. He never touched her, but she somehow felt violated and intimidated by him.

Benny always stayed close, watching, to step in if Jenna needed him. He was beginning to hope that Mr. Parker would make a wrong move, giving him an excuse to do something.

One day Jenna sat at the desk in the entry hall going over the weekly receipts. She felt someone watching her and she looked up from her work. On the stairway stood Harold Parker with a strange smile on his face. Jenna wondered how long he'd been there.

"You don't seem very friendly today, Mrs. McConnell," he stated.

"I'm sorry you feel that way, Mr. Parker." Jenna replied, looking back down at the work in front of her.

"I'm talking to you, Jenna. Look at me when I talk to you!"

The sudden anger in his voice startled her, but she didn't look up.

"I know you could be friendlier, a lot friendlier!"

She ignored the remark and walked into the dining room where Roberto was checking on the buffet. Jenna had always been proud of the fact that she could hold her own with most people. But Harold Parker had her rattled and she hated the feeling.

Jenna didn't tell Tim about the situation. She knew he'd make a scene and she didn't want to embarrass Mrs. Parker, who seemed like a very nice person. Jenna felt sorry for her, married to that strange man.

By the last day of their stay, Jenna was a nervous wreck, jumpy and edgy. *This must be what sexual harassment is about*, she thought. She had never been treated like this before. She wasn't sure how to handle it. *Just one more day, then they'll be gone forever. Things will be back to normal tomorrow,* she thought.

That evening, Jenna lay in the hammock making last minute notes for the horse show. Tim was inside taking a shower. It was almost dusk and out from the long shadows along the hedge came Mr. Parker. He startled her. Smiling down at her in the hammock, he said in that all too familiar deep voice, "I just wanted to tell you how very much I enjoyed my stay. Now that I know how cozy it is here, I'll be back real soon. I won't bring the wife next time, that way we can spend more time together, maybe right here on your patio. Good night, Jenna." A cold shiver went up her spine as he walked back into the darkness.

"Who was that?" Tim asked from the door as he dried his hair with a towel.

Jenna ran to him. "It was that horrible, Mr. Parker." She finally told him the whole story.

Tim was livid. "Why didn't you tell me? I'd have kicked his ass out of here that very first day."

"Don't do anything rash. He never touched me, it was just the way he talked to me; it really scared me."

"Oh, Jen. I'm so sorry. If I'd only known. Benny should have told me."

"I should have told you. It's not Benny's fault. I asked him not to say anything."

"I'll stay home from work tomorrow and check out the Parkers, personally!" Tim announced decidedly. "You stay in here tomorrow."

They both slept fitfully, but by morning Tim was ready. He called a meeting at dawn. Teddy, Jake, Roberto and Benny sat at the kitchen table, listening to Tim.

"Teddy, you and Jake help Mrs. Parker to the car. Roberto, Benny and I will stay back and get the luggage. We'll have a little talk with Mr. Parker," Tim said. He told them all about Jenna's week.

"I'm sorry Tim. I should have said something, but she asked me not to. I just never thought it would get this far," Benny apologized.

Jake was just plain angry. "That guy should be horse whipped for scaring Jenna like that."

"Now Jake, I promised Jen we wouldn't make a scene in front of Mrs. Parker or any of the other guests. Just follow my lead when they come down to check-out."

Now everyone was a little edgy. Old Jake paced one way and then the other in the entry hall, waiting for the Parkers. Finally, the buzzer rang at the front desk. The Parkers wanted their luggage brought down. Roberto and Benny both went up the stairs, two at a time.

"Good morning Mr. and Mrs. Parker, I hope you had a pleasant stay," Tim said from behind the desk as they walked down the stairs.

"Where's your lovely wife this morning?" asked Mrs. Parker. "I wanted to tell her goodbye."

"Oh, she's doing some errands this morning. She'll be sorry to have missed you," Tim smiled graciously.

He gave the bill to Mr. Parker, who tossed him his credit card. "I'll be coming back through here next month on my way to St. Louis. I might as well make my reservations now. I go through here at least once a month or more. I imagine you'd appreciate my business, way out here in the middle of nowhere. Maybe you could give me a better rate next time."

Benny lunged forward at that remark, but Roberto put his arm out to stop him. Tim just kept smiling, "Sorry, sir, but we're booked solid through Labor Day and beyond. Jake, why don't you and Teddy escort Mrs. Parker to her car. She may want to see the geese on the pond this morning. We'll finish this business with Mr. Parker." Tim's smile faded as he looked directly at Harold Parker, who looked around at the five men. None of them were smiling. Suddenly, Mr. Parker realized that they knew.

Jake and Teddy escorted Mrs. Parker out the door. Tim came out from behind the desk as Harold took a step backward, but Benny and Roberto were right there. "Harold, we're booked solid for the rest of your life. Do you understand what I'm saying?" Tim asked as he got up close and personal with Mr. Parker. "Don't ever come back here again!"

"This is certainly no way to treat a paying guest," Harold said in his regular overbearing tone of voice. "It would be a shame if word got around that your little establishment here was rude to their guests."

"Don't threaten me, Harold! It would be a bigger shame if an executive of your company were accused of harassment, especially if there were witnesses! Goodbye, Harold!"

They were finally gone. Jenna came out from behind the door where she'd been listening to the conversation. "You were wonderful, honey!" she said tearfully. "You were all wonderful."

Glad that the harrowing week was almost over, Jenna went into the dining room to gather the dishes from breakfast. "Oh Jenna, dear!" waved Mrs. Barton from across the room. "I'm almost ready to leave. Would you be a darling and get my bill ready while I finish my coffee?"

"Yes, Mrs. Barton, I'd be happy to." *If you only knew how happy,* Jenna thought as she went back out to the desk. Getting Mrs. Barton and the Parkers out of the house would be a big relief.

After a moment, Mrs. Barton walked by the desk and hurried up the stairs. "Send that dear boy, Benny, up to fetch my bags, will you dear?" she said over her shoulder.

A few moments later, Roberto appeared from the dining room. "Jenna, bad news; I saw Mrs. Barton swipe the silver salt and pepper shakers off the table and put them in her purse. She didn't see me standing at the kitchen door. What do you want me to do?"

Jenna thought, "Nothing, I'll take care of Mrs. Barton."

Shortly, Mrs. Barton came down the stairs carrying her dog, Penelope, who was barking and growling at Benny with the luggage. Jenna handed her the bill.

"I've had a wonderful stay here, dear, but there must be some mistake."

Other guests were coming down the stairs as Jenna said, "No, deary, there's no mistake. I think if you read your statement very closely, you'll understand." At the bottom of the page was the bill for one set of antique sterling silver salt and pepper shakers; $150 plus tax.

Mrs. Barton paid the bill without another word. "Have a wonderful day, dear!" shouted Jenna, smiling as Mrs. Barton, Penelope and Benny went out the door.

Chapter 23

The evening was warm and humid as Tim and Jenna wound their way around the hills and curves, headed toward the lake. Jenna rested her head against the seat, letting her hair blow in the wind, while Tim played with the radio dial in their little convertible. Finally, he settled on a station with what he called, "elevator music". It seemed to fit Jenna's melancholy mood.

He'd never figure her out. Just when they were leaving for a few days of rest and relaxation, she suddenly went from hyperactive preparations to quiet depression as she told Jake and the help goodbye. She hadn't said a word for more that twenty miles and he turned to her now, "Jen, are you all right? I thought you'd be excited about the weekend."

"I am," she said without looking at him.

He turned his attention back to the road and the steady stream of Friday night traffic ahead of him. There were lines of red tail lights ahead and at least a hundred pair of tiny white headlights in the rear view mirror, following along behind them like a trail of ants headed for a picnic.

Friday night after work, everyone headed toward the lake for a weekend of sun and sand. Sunday afternoon, they'd all make the return trip, tired, sunburned and dreading Monday morning at the office.

Billboards advertising water parks, marinas, restaurants and resorts lined the side of the road for more than fifty miles. "That looks like fun," Tim said pointing to the large sign advertising a go-cart track and miniature golf.

"I'm not spending my anniversary chasing a little white ball through a maze!" Jenna barked.

"Well, then what would you like to do?"

"Not that!"

"Okay, okay!" *I've set her off again*, Tim thought.

"You're always telling me not to plan so much; be more spontaneous. Why can't we just play it by ear? I want to sleep in for once. Not have to serve breakfast to everyone else. I want to be served for a change!"

"God, you're sure a grouch! Do you hate our life that much?"

"Yes!" she blurted out, instantly regretting the remark. She looked over at Tim. Now he was depressed, too. Why had she said such a thing? She didn't mean it. She'd hurt him and now she was sorry. *What's the matter with me?* she wondered. *I don't hate our life. I'm just tired of the everyday hassles. I'm tired of the guests constantly interrupting our privacy.*

Tomorrow would be their second anniversary and she was ruining it before it started. She reached across and lovingly rubbed Tim's shoulder. "I'm sorry, that was a terrible thing to say. I don't hate our life. I don't know why I said that.

Tim looked straight ahead, "Freudian slip, maybe?" he asked quietly.

"No, not at all, I'm just stressed out."

"What do you want me to do? Do you want me to quit my job? Close the office and take more responsibility of the Inn?"

"No," she answered, tears brimming in her eyes. "You love your job."

"What then? What can I do? Do you want me to hire a full-time bookkeeper, more help and more waitresses? What?" He was angry now, tired of playing the "Poor Jenna" game.

A car suddenly cut them off and Tim laid on the horn, "You jerk!" he yelled at the driver. The car load of teenagers was laughing, giving Tim hand gestures and he was getting furious. He speeded up and got as close to their bumper as he could. They passed the car ahead and so did Tim, narrowly escaping the van coming toward them.

"Tim, don't go so fast!" Jenna yelled. She'd never seen him like this before. The faster the teenagers went, the faster Tim went, tailgating all the way, only inches from the bumper. They passed cars going around curves and up hills. "You're going to kill somebody!" she yelled.

Finally, they met a highway patrol car and Tim slowed down. He could feel his heart pounding in his neck. "Sorry," he said, still not looking at her.

They didn't speak the rest of the way. The stars and the full moon hung low in the sky, their silver reflections rippling out in the waves across the lake as the little convertible drove along the shoreline to the resort. They could feel the tension in the air on this gorgeous evening, so much like the night they had arrived for their honeymoon.

Their wedding had been beautiful, a warm sunny late afternoon in June. The gardens had been a kaleidoscope of color against the little gazebo decorated with wildflowers and long flowing satin ribbons. The guests were seated in folding chairs in rows along the stone pathway.

Jake proudly walked from stone to stone with Jenna beside him. He was nervous that day and she squeezed his arm, smiling at him, telling him it was okay.

Tim and the minister waited ahead, flanked by Curt, Tom and Trent on their left and Sarah, Keri and Samantha on their right. Everyone was looking at Jenna. Her hair was piled high on her head, curly tendrils cascading down over her wildflower headpiece. Her long gown of satin and lace flowed like liquid along the ground. All Jenna could see was Tim.

He looked so handsome in his tuxedo smiling at her as she came closer. She loved him so much. For a brief moment, she wished her parents were alive to know Tim. They would have liked him. *If only they could have been here*, she thought. *Maybe they are*, she finally decided.

Harp music floated out across the yard as the pastor pronounced them, man and wife. The guests were clapping as Tim kissed her and they started back towards the Inn, to the sound of "Clair de lune".

From the corner of her eye, Jenna saw Sarah crying into a lace handkerchief. Tim's mother was crying, too. Jenna hoped they were tears of joy, not sorrow. Faces blurred as she and Tim hurried down the path and into the house.

Roberto had outdone himself. The cake was a work of art. Tim swiped his finger across the bottom layer and shared the creamy fluff with Jenna. Roberto frowned at them and then carefully repaired his creation.

They danced all evening in the ballroom, which had been transformed with flowers, satin streamers and balloons. Still in their beautiful dresses, Keri and Samantha danced barefoot with Benny, while Curt, Tom and Trent fought over Jenna's garter that Tim had flung into their waiting hands.

The guests lingered quite late, everyone having a great time. Finally, Tim and Jenna sneaked down the stairs, out through the back door and down the path to the little guest cottage. "Wait," Jenna said as she stopped halfway from the house. "My dream was that you'd carry me to our cottage in the woods."

"Well, if you say so," Tim replied, as he faked a bad "war injury" and held his back. They laughed as he struggled along, nearly dropping her as he tried to open the door.

The next evening, Jenna yelled out the car window on their way to the lake, "Life is good; life is complete. I love you, Timothy McConnell!" The same stars twinkled along the shore to the resort for the rest of their honeymoon. It had been perfect. The week had gone by so quickly, and they were surprised that it was time to head back to work.

Now, as they sat silently side by side, Jenna remembered how in love they had been just two years before on this same road, under the same moon. Would they ever feel that close again? Were they slowly drifting apart? It was all her fault, and she knew it. How could she start over? How could she make it up to Tim for her grumpy, irritable moods? She knew she was being bitchy, but she couldn't seem to stop.

"Tim, let's make a pact. Let's start our second honeymoon right now. Let's forget the last few weeks. I'm sorry I've been so cranky. I'll do better, I promise!"

Tim pulled into a parking area that overlooked the lake. He shut off the engine, got out of the car and opened her door, pulling her into his arms. He kissed her gently and told her he loved her. They sat down on a bench nearby and looked out across the lake, the lights from a marina on the other shore, shimmered out across the water toward them.

"This was just what we needed; peace and quiet." Tim looked up at the stars and took a deep breath. Jenna rested her head on his shoulder and relaxed for the first time in months.

Chapter 24

"Is Jenna upset again?" Teddy asked Tim as they loaded the last steer into the livestock trailer, with Jake supervising.

"How did you know?" Tim asked.

"You're out here with me when I didn't even ask 'ya, that's how."

"She was just fine at the lake. We went sailing and dancing, all the things she wanted to. I thought everything was better. Then, the minute we got back, she started crying because Roberto was out of potatoes; potatoes! I don't know what to think. This morning she got sick when she smelled bacon cooking in the kitchen and then, started to cry. Go figure!"

"Maybe she's pregnant. Annie got sick every morning before Marisa was born," Jake declared.

The three men looked at each other. "That might explain the mood swings," Tim added. "Wouldn't that be something?"

"Hormone unbalanced," Teddy stated seriously.

"What? Did you say hormone unbalanced? Now what would you know about hormone imbalance?" Tim asked, having a hard time keeping a straight face. "An older gentleman like yourself, I mean."

"I heard it on television. Jus' cause I ain't married, don't mean I don't know woman stuff. I seen it on one of them ladies talk shows," Teddy replied.

"Okay then, it must be so," teased Tim. "I'll go tell Jen your theory.

"You go right ahead. She'll know what I mean," Teddy said with certainty.

Tim went toward the house, trying not to laugh out loud. He found Jenna in the kitchen washing dishes. "Don't come in here with those dirty boots on. Who knows what you've stepped in?" Jenna barked.

"Jen, wait until you hear what Jake and Teddy think," laughed Tim as he tried to ignore the boot remark. "They think you're pregnant!"

Tears welled up in her eyes as she replied, "So do I. I haven't been to the doctor yet, but I think I might be. Would you be upset if it's true?"

"Oh, Jen, I'd be thrilled. Would you be upset?"

"No, but we really hadn't planned it this soon," she said trying not to cry.

"Some things in life just aren't planned, Hon; at least not by us. I told you that we need to be more spontaneous," he said as he held her in his arms.

"I think being so 'spontaneous' might be what got us here in the first place, don't you?" she asked as she smiled up at him.

"That, or hormone unbalanced," Tim laughed.

"What?" she asked.

Chapter 25

"A Christmas baby would be wonderful!" Sarah exclaimed, while the rest of the group all clapped and cheered. Tim and Jenna's baby was due in late December or early January.

"A new baby and a new year; what could be better?" Tim exclaimed shaking hands with Jake and Teddy.

"Well, we'd better get back to work," Jenna said, "We just wanted to share the news with all of you at the same time.

The Inn was busy through the summer and before they knew it, the leaves started to change color out through the hills. The days were getting shorter and winter was on its way. Jenna's little tummy was getting bigger by the day and she could no longer get out of the hammock alone. In fact, even the couch was beginning to become a challenge.

Tim patted her tummy and talked to the baby every chance he had. He read, played music and sang as he laid his head on Jenna's lap. "What are you doing?" Jenna asked as she heard Tim whisper to the baby.

"I'm just telling him the baseball scores. If it's a boy, he should know these things."

"What if it's a girl?"

"If it's a girl, she's probably doing her nails and isn't paying attention to me, anyway!" They both laughed. Jenna was feeling much better now and seemed happier than she'd been in a long time.

"I feel great," she told Sarah one day as they reviewed the ledgers, "but I think I'm losing my mind. Can being pregnant affect your brain?"

"Why?" she asked laughing.

"I seem to be losing all kinds of things lately."

"Like what?"

"Oh, nothing important, just little things like some old baby pictures of me, stuff like that. I can't find them anywhere."

"Maybe one of the guests has them?"

"Who would swipe my baby pictures? Besides, nobody goes into our apartment. I'll find them. I've evidently just misplaced them. They'll turn up. They've got to be here somewhere, don't they?"

Jenna had looked everywhere for the pictures. She wanted them for an album she was putting together for the baby. The page entitled, "Mommy's baby picture" was conspicuously empty, while "Daddy's baby picture" showed Tim's smiling face covered with what looked like chocolate pudding at the age of six months.

Jim and Lisa had been thrilled when Tim called with the news about the baby. The very next day, Lisa had sent pictures and old baby clothes of Tim's.

When they arrived, Jenna opencd the box and held up a tiny blue sweater.

"Did you put my sweater in the dryer, again?" asked Tim.

"No, Smarty, but this is yours. Isn't it cute?"

"What can I say; I always was a snappy dresser."

"I wish I'd kept my baby clothes."

"Why didn't you?"

"I guess when my folks died, I was in shock. I just couldn't handle going through all of their personal things. I had an auctioneer come and get everything that would sell and dispose of the rest. I was just a kid and needed the money. Does that sound terrible to you? I wish now that I had kept things. I just didn't think I could deal with it at the time. I didn't even go to the sale. I couldn't bear it."

"Is that why you didn't want Jake to be alone on the day of the auction?" Tim asked, suddenly understanding.

"I was alone the day of my parents' sale. I sat on the floor in our empty house and cried. I had no idea what I was going to do. I was lost and alone, with no place to go. Just as I thought there was no hope for me, Jake and Annie came through the door. They gathered me up from the floor, helped me pack my clothes and took me home to live with them. I never dreamed someday I'd be a mom. I just wish I could find those pictures. I had them right here, I know I did. It's like they've just vanished.

"They'll show up. We'll get the staff to keep a look out for them, too. You probably laid them down someplace and forgot. No problem."

But, they didn't find the precious pictures Jenna had treasured all those years. Several weeks went by with no trace of them. Then, one morning while the cleaning crew was at work, Clara, a neighbor who often helped out, found a pile of partially burned photos in the fireplace of the suite.

"Who would do such a thing?" Jenna asked as she tried to brush away the crusty brown edges of the pictures. They were crisp and even a gentle touch made the paper crumble in her hands. She laid them down carefully on the coffee table in the apartment. Tears rolled down her cheeks as she realized that the ones of her father holding her were still missing. "They must have burned completely. Without those pictures, our baby will never see my dad's rugged and wonderful face. I can barely remember it myself. I can't remember his eyes. I just can't remember them."

"Calm down, Jen. You'll remember, you're just upset right now. Jake knew your dad and he'll help you. Don't cry, honey."

Jenna was sad and suddenly depressed again. The next few days went by her in a blur. Everyone was trying to cheer her up, but without much success.

Tim sang sweet, funny songs to the baby with his head in Jenna's lap in front of the television. She bent down to kiss him, which was no longer an easy task, but her thoughts were far away. Her beautiful smile was gone.

Trying to help, Sarah came over with a small, fuzzy teddy bear for the baby and a hug for Jenna.

I've got to snap out of this, Jenna said to herself as she placed the little bear in a corner of the crib that she and Tim had put together a few days earlier. *Snap out of it and move on,* she thought as she smoothed out the soft pink and blue sheets decorated with tiny lambs.

178

"Is that a smile I see?" asked Tim as he peeked into the room. "Is that our sweet little mommy here again?"

"Yes, I've decided to shape up and get on with things," Jenna stated, determined to do better.

But, two days later as Jenna walked past the door of the baby's room, she noticed that the little bear was missing from the crib. *Had Tim moved it*, she wondered? After a quick search of the apartment and a frantic phone call to Tim's office, Jenna called Jake and the help together in the kitchen. "The baby's new teddy bear is missing. Have any of you seen it?" They all looked at each other.

"I didn't take it," Teddy announced.

"Oh, Teddy, I'm not accusing anyone of taking it. I just don't know where it could be."

"I need to get back to work," Benny stated, obviously disgusted that he had come inside for this. "I'm trying to winterize the cottage. Can I go now?"

"I'm sorry; I shouldn't have bothered all of you. You must think I'm losing my mind." No one said a word as Jenna walked out to the front desk, shaking her head. *What's happening? I'm getting paranoid*, she thought to herself. *Why would anyone steal a teddy bear?* She could understand if it was an expensive antique, but a new toy?

She tried to put it out of her head as she checked in new guests and served tea and cookies to a group of ladies in the solarium.

Later that week, Jenna rushed to Tim as he came home from work. "Tim, someone is taking things from our apartment. Now I

179

can't find your baby sweater or the bear. I'm getting scared. I feel like someone is watching me. When I was in the cellar today, I saw a flash from the corner of my eye. It was like someone was taking pictures. It's creepy."

"Jen, calm down. I'll go down and look around," Tim said as he helped her sit down on the couch. "You're just getting yourself all worked up for nothing."

"Don't go down there, please, don't go. Tim, I know someone is in this house."

"Honey, lots of people are in the house. No one is going to hurt you. Just relax. I'll be right back." Tim opened the cellar door and went down the steps. Everything seemed to be in place. Could someone really be hiding down here? His mind raced and suddenly he remembered the tiny room under the solarium. He took the flashlight that Jake used when he gave his tour and peered into the darkness. The flashlight spread its beam out across the old dirt floor and up the crumbling walls to the ceiling. *No one here.* Tim thought to himself. As he moved the light back to the floor, he caught a glimpse of something in the far corner. Carefully, he went towards it, as a sudden chill ran up his spine. His tiny blue baby sweater lay shredded in the corner.

He looked down at the dirt floor. Next to his feet were footprints in the dirt. Someone had been here and recently, by the looks of it. He hurried up the steps and called the sheriff.

Chapter 26

Sheriff Kinard was a fifty-something, chubby little man, who's integrity was above reproach. He listened carefully as Jenna and Tim explained the events of the past few weeks.

"It just doesn't make any sense, Sheriff. The items that are missing or destroyed don't have any value, except to us. We just can't figure it out." Tim said as he held Jenna's hand. They sat side-by-side on the couch in the apartment. The shredded sweater and parched photos lay on the coffee table in front of them.

"I don't mean to scare you, Mrs. McConnell, but it looks to me that someone is trying to frighten you for some reason," the sheriff stated as he paced back and forth across the room. "I'll need a detailed list of the things that are missing. I want you to look through everything. Maybe there are things missing that you haven't discovered yet. Also, I'll need a list of everyone who's had access to the suite, your apartment and the basement. Don't forget anyone; guests, employees, delivery people, plumbers, electricians, anyone." He hesitated, "I'll also need the names of anyone who might have a grudge against you; disgruntled employees, old boyfriends <u>or girlfriends</u>, for that matter, Tim. Don't forget family members, either."

Jenna and Tim looked at each other.

"Oh, I know what you're going to say, but often times it's someone very close to you," the sheriff paced, trying to think. "Anyone you've ever thrown out of here?"

Jenna shot up, "Harold Parker, that guy from Omaha, last summer. He was creepy and really upset when he left."

"That was months ago, Jen," Tim stated.

"Don't worry about that. Often a grudge goes on for some length of time before anyone acts upon it. Write it all down. I'm going to take a look around. Show me the basement, Tim, I want to see those footprints," the sheriff announced, as he walked to the door. "Do you keep this door locked most of the time?"

They shook their heads.

"I'd lock it if I were you."

Now Tim was frightened. Who on earth would want to hurt Jenna. None in their right mind, that's for sure. He stopped in his tracks. The words "in their right mind" suddenly had new meaning to him.

*   *   *

Jenna sat at her desk in the den, trying to think of people with access to the house. Jake came in and sat down in the big leather chair across from her.

"Can I help, Jenna?" Jake asked quietly. "I hate this for you."

"Yes, you can help. I need the names of anyone who ever stepped foot in this house in the past several years."

"You're kidding, I hope."

"No, especially people who disliked me. I've got a list of guests and their addresses, but the only one I can think of with a grudge is Harold Parker." Tears came to her eyes and Jake went to her and put his arms around her. "Oh, Jake, I'm so scared. Could someone hate me that much?"

"No one hates you, Jenna, no one. Everyone loves you." He held her and comforted her like he did when she was a child. Sometimes she took care of him and sometimes he took care of her.

*   *   *

The sheriff left with several lists and encouraged them to keep thinking. He promised to check out Harold Parker and said he'd return to question others on the list, including Jake.

That evening, Tim announced, "There is no way Uncle Jake could be involved. Teddy, Roberto and Benny have been here since the beginning. They all love you." Tim sighed as he tried to eliminate people from the lists.

"What about Ellen?" Jenna asked. "I know that didn't end as well as it might have."

"Don't be ridiculous. Ellen doesn't even know you. She moved on from that long ago." Tim answered, a little angry that she would even think of such a thing. "What about the good doctor? He's never particularly liked the idea of us being together. Maybe he's drinking again."

"Stop right there. He would never hurt me; never. Don't even suggest Chuck to Sheriff Kinard. That kind of accusation could ruin his practice. Promise me you won't say a word about him."

The sheriff was at the Inn at 7:30 the next morning, questioning Jake, Benny, Roberto and the cleaning crew. One by one they each marched into the den for the third degree and came out frustrated and angry. There was tension in the air and two weeks went by with cold stares and solemn faces. Everyone felt like a suspect and just when Jenna needed them the most, they all distanced themselves from her. They were hurt that she had put their names on the list. Even poor, old Teddy had been questioned.

Jenna was miserable. The baby was kicking half the night and when she could finally fall asleep, she was having nightmares.

"Hon, you have to get some rest for yourself and the baby." Tim was getting concerned.

The sheriff called to say that a friend of his in the Omaha Police Department had agreed to check out Harold Parker. "Other than Parker, I really have no other strong suspect," he admitted. "I can't do much until something serious happens. Harassment is tough to prove. It's a fine line that gets crossed every day. Maybe we've scared whoever it was, away. Sometimes just telling the authorities is enough to stop them. Let me know if anything else happens. Hopefully, it's over."

"It might be over for him," Jenna told Tim, "but it's not over with the help. I have to talk to each of them. I have to explain why they were on the lists. I can't stand them being angry with me anymore."

One by one Jenna explained why they had to be questioned. "The sheriff made me produce a list with everyone who had access to the house. I never once suspected any of you, but the sheriff had to ask questions, without me interfering. I hate that he made you feel like a suspect. I knew you would never hurt me like that," she told Roberto and Benny. "Please forgive me. I told the sheriff it wasn't either of you, but he had to ask anyway."

"It's okay, Jenna," Roberto replied. "I understand the circumstances, but it was a little intimidating to be questioned like that. We didn't know what to think."

"What about you, Benny?" Jenna asked.

Without saying a word, Benny turned and went out the door, slamming it behind him.

"He'll get over it," Roberto said. "He's had a crush on you ever since he got here. You must have known that. It hurt him to be questioned. I think it sort of broke his spirit. He hasn't said much since, but he'll get over it," Roberto said as he went back to his pastry dough. Jenna watched out the window as Benny drove away.

Now she felt worse than before. "Broke his spirit," the words rang in her ears. She hadn't realized that Benny had a crush on her. He was always there when she needed him and now his heart was broken. She had to find him and tell him how sorry she was.

She waddled to the door. "Where do you think you're going?" Roberto asked, hands on his hips.

"I'm going after him; I've got to make him understand."

"Oh, no you're not! I've got strict instructions from Tim to make sure you rest all day today. Now go and get off of your feet. That's an order, lady!" Roberto helped her through the narrow pantry and into the apartment, where he settled her onto the couch. He kissed the top of her head and smiled down at her.

"Thanks," she said, glad that the tension seemed over between them. She tried to lay back and rest, but the thought of Benny somewhere alone, bothered her. She called Sarah.

"I need a huge favor."

"What's that?" asked Sarah.

"Would you please go to Benny's apartment and see if he's there? I really need to talk to him. This whole situation has really upset him. Ask him to come back and talk to me, would you please?"

Sarah left the store, putting a trusted customer in charge and hurried over to Benny's apartment. His car was in the driveway, but he didn't answer the door. She could see him through the window. She turned the knob and went inside.

"Benny, are you all right?" she asked. "Jenna needs to talk to you."

She had startled him. Benny whirled around, holding the missing teddy bear and a half-burned photo of Jenna's father. There was a blank expression on his face.

Sarah looked around the room. There were pictures of the pregnant Jenna everywhere. She gasped, "You're the stalker! Do you have any idea how much you've scared Jenna? She's terrified. She trusted you; how could you do this to her?"

Benny ran past her and down the steps, still clutching the picture and the bear.

Sarah ran directly to the phone and called Sheriff Kinard. "Benny is the stalker," she yelled into the phone. "Go to the Inn right away, he may try to hurt Jenna." She hung up the phone before the sheriff could say anything. She had to call Jenna to warn her. The line was busy. She waited for what seemed like forever and tried again, still busy. *I can't wait*, she thought. *I have to get there before he does something crazy.*

Sarah ran down the steps and rushed to her car. She hurried down the road toward the Inn. As she turned the corner, she could see smoke coming out of the windows on the north side of the house. *Oh, no, Tim and Jenna's apartment*, she thought.

The guests were rushing out the front door and she could hear the smoke alarms screaming as she pulled up to the back of the house. Jake, Teddy and Roberto were standing outside the kitchen door. "Where's Jenna?" she yelled.

Just then, Benny burst out the door carrying Jenna in his arms. He handed her to Roberto and rushed back into the Inn. Smoke came from the kitchen windows as they just stood there in shock.

From a distance came the sounds of sirens. Two fire trucks and several deputies arrived at the same time. The fire chief hurriedly asked, "Is everyone out?"

"No," Jenna yelled above the noise, "Benny!"

Just then, Benny came through the smoke, clutching the baby book. Sheriff Kinard stepped out and grabbed him.

"You're under arrest for stalking and possible attempted murder and arson if you started this fire." He yanked Benny's arm behind his back and slapped on handcuffs.

Jenna couldn't believe her eyes. She ran to Benny. "He didn't do this, he saved my life! You've got the wrong person!"

"No, Jenna, Benny is the stalker. I have proof," Sarah offered.

Jenna glanced up at him. He couldn't look into her eyes. "Oh, Benny, not you!" Sarah grabbed the book away from him, as Sheriff Kinard read him his rights.

Firemen dragged the heavy hoses into the house. Smoke was billowing out the windows of the apartment. One of the paramedics checked Jenna's heart and lungs and then decided to take her to the hospital to check on the baby.

Chapter 27

The Fire Marshall had finished his investigation and found evidence of arson. The Inn was closed for repairs. There had been smoke and water damage to the apartment and the rest of the house would have to be thoroughly cleaned before it could reopen.

Tim and Jenna were staying at Sarah's house, while Jake was living in the loft with Teddy. It had been three days since the fire, but Jenna was still living in denial.

"I can't believe it, I can't believe Benny would try to hurt me. He saved me. He knew I couldn't hurry, so he carried me out of the house. He would never try to kill me."

"Jenna, how many times do I have to tell you? I caught him red-handed with your pictures and the teddy bear. His apartment looks like a shrine to "St. Jenna". There are pictures of you everywhere. He's totally obsessed with you!" Sarah exclaimed. "Stop defending him."

"That fire could have killed you and the baby. All the guests were in danger, too." Tim explained. "I don't know what he was trying to do, but it hurt all of us."

"I'm fine, the baby's fine. The Inn will reopen in a few weeks. I'm not going to file charges against him for stalking. I just don't believe he would ever hurt me," Jenna announced firmly.

"You're being naïve. I'll file charges, if you don't. There's just too much evidence.

"Tim, I'm going over to the jail. I want to hear his side of the story."

"You're not going anywhere! I'll talk to him," Tim replied. "It will be pretty hard to deny it with all the pictures they found in his room. The jail is no place for you right now. I'll find out what was going on with him, one way or another."

"Let him explain. There has to be an explanation and try to keep an open mind, please Tim."

"I'll try, but he has nearly destroyed everything we have."

"We still have each other."

"Okay, I'll listen to him, but prepare yourself. You may be unpleasantly surprised by what I find out."

*   *   *

The county jail was small and the visitor's room looked more like a closet. Tim sat at a square metal table waiting for the guard to bring Benny in. "He hasn't got enough money for a lawyer, so the judge will appoint a public defender tomorrow. I told him he didn't have to talk to you, but he wants to. You have ten minutes," explained the guard.

Benny looked as if he had aged ten years in the past three days. "How's Jenna? Is the baby okay?" Benny asked as soon as the guard left the room.

"Do you care?" Tim asked angrily.

"Of course I care, Tim. I didn't start that fire, I swear. I would never hurt Jenna, or anyone else for that matter."

"What about the pictures and the teddy bear; can you explain that?"

"I have only ten minutes to tell you this. It's very important. I know you don't believe me, but I can explain. Please hear me out."

"Start explaining."

"I did take the baby pictures of Jenna and her dad." Tim got out of his chair and went toward the door. "Wait, I took them because he was my dad, too. I'm Jenna's brother. I'd never seen him and I needed to see what he looked like."

"What?" Tim asked as he sat back down. "You're her brother?"

"Her half-brother; my mother had an affair about twenty five years ago. He didn't want anything to do with me when I was born. He paid my mom to go away and leave him alone. She did for the first five years. We went to Arkansas and lived with my grandfather, but he didn't like me either because mom wasn't married. We were a disgrace to her family and he finally threw us out. So, we moved back here. One night, mom confronted Jenna's parents in Blakesburg. She told Jen's mother about the affair and that she had a five year old son to prove it: me! Jenna's mother was furious. She ran to their car and tried to drive away, but Jenna's dad; my dad," he explained sadly, "got in the passenger door and they sped off."

Benny took a deep breath, "The highway patrol found their car in the ditch. Both of them were dead."

Tim sat there stunned.

"Mom found out about the accident the next day. We left town and went to Oklahoma. The only thing I can actually remember is her crying. She cried all the time when I was young. If I asked about my father, she'd shake her head and cry. So, I finally quit asking."

Benny went on, "Mom died about four years ago and I had no one. After her funeral, the lawyer gave me a letter. It told me the whole story, who my father was, everything. I came here to find out more about him. I asked in town if anyone knew if he had children. They told me Jenna was his only child. I came to the Inn to talk to her, but she thought I came about the bellhop job. So, I said I needed a job, and she hired me. The better I got to know her, the harder it was for me to tell her."

"When Jenna showed me her baby pictures, I saw my father holding her. At first, I just wanted to get copies made. I waited for her to leave the apartment and I went in to get them. I heard her coming in from the patio, so I grabbed them all and hurried out. I never meant to upset her. I was afraid she'd hate me if I told her about my mom, so I hid the pictures. I decided I should burn some of them so she'd never suspect me of taking them."

"She was getting so upset, I decided I should leave and never tell her. But I started taking pictures of her when she wasn't looking. I wanted to take them with me when I left. I decided I'd leave so she'd never know that our father had been unfaithful."

"What about the teddy bear, why take that?" Tim asked.

"I know this sounds weird, but the baby she's carrying is my niece or nephew. I knew if I left, I'd never get to see the baby, so I took the teddy bear. I just wanted something to remember. I'm so sorry it frightened Jenna."

"So tell me this; why my baby sweater?" Tim interrupted.

"I don't know anything about the sweater. The cops keep asking me, but I don't know what they're talking about. You have to believe me, Tim."

"Benny, I just don't know about all this."

"Tim, listen to me. I did not start that fire. If it was arson, someone else is trying to hurt Jenna."

"I found the baby sweater in the cellar all shredded up in the corner of the old slave room. Are you telling me you didn't do that?" Tim asked.

"Believe me Tim, it wasn't me. Tim, I swear!" Benny was shaking and crying, clutching the front of Tim's shirt from across the table.

Tim did believe him. "I'll get you a good lawyer. We'll straighten this all out with the sheriff, but I need to get home to Jenna to warn her that she may still be in danger." Tim hurried out to his car and phoned Sarah's house.

"Hello."

"Sarah, I need to talk to Jen!"

"What's the matter?"

"I'll explain later, where is she?"

"She just left for the Inn to salvage some of her maternity clothes."

"Oh, God, no!" Tim replied as he turned off the cell phone.

Chapter 28

Jenna unlocked the kitchen entrance to the Inn. The overpowering stench of smoke nauseated her as she opened the door. Everything in the kitchen looked in order, but the clay tile floor was muddy from the fire hoses and a greasy black film was on everything.

She went through the narrow pantry under the stairs and into the apartment. It was totally dark. The windows had been boarded up by the firemen. She felt her way along the wall toward the light switch, but the electricity had been turned off.

Her eyes were slowly adjusting to the dim light coming through the sides of the temporary repairs. She could make out a flashlight on the mantle across the room. She turned it on. The living room was eerie. The walls and ceiling were black, the furniture scorched and soggy.

She made her way toward the bedroom to look for what was left of her clothes. Suddenly, Jenna felt the presence of someone behind her. She turned around slowly, afraid of what she might see. Her heart was pounding. It was Harold Parker, smiling that strange, evil smile. He had a knife in his right hand.

Just then the phone rang on the table near the couch. Jenna lunged for it. Harold brought the knife down onto her hand. She screamed and dropped the receiver on the floor. "Don't hurt me! Don't hurt my baby!" she pleaded.

"You little bitch! You've ruined my life and now I'm going to ruin yours!" Harold Parker stared at her with raw hatred. "The police came to my office and accused me of harassing you. They thought I'd stolen items from the Inn. They asked questions about me from the office staff. They searched my desk and even went to my home. I was fired the next day and now my wife has left me. It's all your fault! You've taken everything from me and now I'm going to take everything from you!"

Jenna was crying, holding her bloody hand. Suddenly she grabbed her tummy and cried out in pain. "It's the baby! I'm having contractions!"

"Oh, don't give me that crap! You're not having the baby!"

"I am, I really am!" she pleaded. "I'm sorry you lost your job. I'm sorry your wife left you. I won't tell anyone about this. The sheriff thinks Benny started the fire. You're off the hook. Let me go and I promise I won't tell anyone."

Her hand was throbbing now and bleeding badly. She didn't know which hurt more, the contractions or her wound. Her heart was racing and she knew she needed to stay calm for the baby. *God help me*, she prayed silently. *Tell me what to do.*

"I'm going to finish the job I started. This place will burn to the ground with you and your 'precious' baby in it," Harold yelled as he picked up a small can of gasoline and threw it on her.

She turned away, but the gas trickled down her arm and burned as it hit the cut on her hand. The odor made her eyes water and she coughed as the fumes burned her throat. She started to back away from him, but he grabbed her bloody hand and pulled it behind her back. He raised the cold blade of the knife to her throat.

Her mind raced, she had to think of something. Another contraction was starting and she let out a blood-curdling scream, and grabbed the flashlight on the mantle next to her. Harold hit it out of her hand and it rolled across the floor and broke.

The sudden darkness startled Harold and he loosened his grip ever so slightly. It was just enough for Jenna to break his grasp. She ran through the pantry, knocking over boxes and pans as she went. He followed close behind. Jenna could hear the sound of the knife slicing through the air as he came toward her. She threw a heavy crockery bowl at him, but he ducked.

Her legs felt like rubber as she tried to get to the kitchen. It was as if everything was in slow motion. As she burst through the kitchen, a hand reached out and grabbed her. It was Tim.

The sheriff and two deputies stepped between her and Harold, their guns drawn. Harold dropped the knife and held up his hands, "Don't shoot!" he pleaded. "It's her fault, it's all her fault!"

"The ambulance is on the way, Jen. They'll be here in a minute," Tim said as he set her at the kitchen table. He grabbed a towel from a drawer and wrapped it tightly around her hand. "It's all right, honey; everything is going to be all right."

She was suddenly very dizzy and she could feel herself passing out. She could hear the voices of the paramedics and Tim telling her to hang on, but she couldn't open her eyes. The voices seemed so far away. Everything went black.

Chapter 29

Baby Girl McConnell, seven pounds, five ounces, read the card on the hospital bassinet.

Tim was holding Jenna's bandaged hand when she finally woke up. "Hi, sweetheart. You really had us scared," he said quietly as he kissed her cheek. "We have a beautiful baby girl and she has a very brave mommy."

Jenna looked around the room. She was in the hospital, hooked up to monitors and IVs. "What happened?" she asked.

"You were unconscious when the paramedics arrived. They got you here as fast as they could, but you had lost a lot of blood and the baby was in distress. They had to take her. I was there when she was born. Oh, Jen, she's so perfect. She looks just like you."

"Can I see her?"

"Soon, honey, very soon," Tim whispered. "Go back to sleep. You need your rest. They'll bring her in to see you in just a little while."

Tim spent the next hour with his nose pressed against the window of the hospital nursery, proudly watching his tiny baby sleep, stretch and yawn. He was positive that he'd seen her smile, but another father quickly pointed out it was just gas. But, Tim knew for sure it was a smile.

He was sitting on the edge of Jenna's bed when the nurse finally brought their little girl in to visit mommy. Jenna smiled when she was placed into her arms. "You're right Tim, she's perfect." He held them both close to him and prayed that he would never again come so close to losing them.

Sheriff Kinard came to the door of Jenna's room. She was sleeping now and Tim quietly got up from his chair next to her and went out in the hallway to talk to him.

"How is she?"

"She's doing pretty well for the circumstances," Tim replied.

"I came to tell you what we found out about Parker. It seems he's been accused of harassment over the years by several women. Since his arrest, two more from his office have come forward. I've charged him with assault with a deadly weapon, attempted murder and arson. When Jenna dropped the phone, we were all able to hear his confession. Good thing we were already on our way out there when you called her. If you hadn't convinced me that Benny was innocent and that Jenna was still in danger, no telling what might have happened. I'm not sure if the doctors will let him go to trial or not. He's a strange dude! Seems he has a history of mental illness. One way or another, he'll be put away for a very long time. I just wanted you to know."

"Thanks, sheriff," Tim said with relief as they shook hands. "Come with me, I want to introduce you to my daughter."

The next day a parade of people came through the door. Sarah was first, bearing gifts and asking to hold the little one. Then entered

Roberto with Jenna's favorite pastry, explaining that he was sure the hospital was not feeding her right. Jake and Teddy were close behind, neither brave enough to hold the baby when Jenna offered.

"What's her name?" Jake asked as he smiled down at the sweet little bundle in Jenna's arms.

"We've wanted to talk to you about that," Tim replied. "Would it be all right if we named her Annebelle?"

"All right? I'd be proud!" Jake answered with misty eyes.

"Annebelle Marie McConnell, meet your family," Jenna stated with pride. "Marie was my mother's name."

Little Annie Marie opened one eye then closed it again, not particularly liking all the bright lights.

"She winked at me," Teddy announced.

"She's only 36 hours old and she's already flirting with the boys," Tim replied with a smile.

*   *   *

Jenna had been asking questions about Benny and Harold Parker, but Tim kept putting her off, stalling for time. "Jen, this is our time with Annie. I'll tell you about everything else when you're stronger. Benny is okay. I'm not filing charges. He said to give you his love. He can hardly wait to see the baby."

"But, Tim…" Jenna pleaded.

"Later, honey, later."

Jenna was getting stronger every day, but before they left, the hospital psychologist warned that they had been through a very traumatic situation. Jenna would have to take one day at a time. "You've been through a lot these past few weeks; the fire, the stalking, the assault, the baby and all you have ahead of you. Go slow, Jenna," he cautioned. "I'm just a phone call away if you need to talk. Remember, go slow and everything will fall into place. Don't rush to judgment."

What did he mean, don't rush to judgment?

Crews were working on cleaning the Inn as Tim and Jenna drove up the drive with little Annie Marie. The suite and the kitchen were finished, but the Inn wouldn't be open for months. Jenna wanted to spend the first few days at home, with just Tim and the baby.

"Things are a mess. Are you sure you don't want to stay with Sarah for awhile?" Tim asked as he stepped over a ladder and guided Jenna around several buckets in the entry hall.

"I want to be here. I need to be here and so does Annie," Jenna declared firmly.

"Okay, but don't blame me if you break your neck stumbling through this mess to the kitchen for that three a.m. feeding."

"That's the beauty of my plan. You'll be the one stumbling to the kitchen at three," she smiled. "Won't you, daddy?"

Little Annie Marie slept soundly in the new crib that Tim had put together the day before. "Isn't she something?" Tim asked as he and Jenna stood watching their tiny baby breathe in and out. "This is better than TV!"

"She truly is a miracle. I can't believe she's our very own child, Tim. We finally have our own little family."

"Speaking of family, Jen," he hesitated. "There's something I need to tell you, something I've been keeping from you."

"You're scaring me," she replied, trying to brace herself for bad news. "I knew there was something more to this whole nightmare. I could sense it. Tell me, I need to know what really happened."

Tim sat her down beside him on the bed next to the crib. "This may be very painful for you to hear. I'm not sure you're ready."

"Tim, don't do this, I have to know. Tell me."

Slowly and as gently as he knew how, he recounted the entire conversation he had with Benny at the jail. Jenna didn't say a word. She listened in shock. She mourned for her mother, knowing how much pain she must have felt that terrible night of the accident. She had been betrayed by the man she loved and now Jenna felt somehow betrayed, too. Her father, the love of her life, had been unfaithful to her mother.

Tim could see the hurt in her eyes. "Jen, I'm sure your father loved you very much, just the way we love Annie. Whatever was going on between your mom and your dad, it didn't have anything to do with how they felt about you."

"Tell me about Benny." Jenna said quietly, never taking her eyes off little Annie's precious face.

"The day you hired him, he was actually coming to confront you. He took the job instead, and over time he couldn't help but love you. He has loved you from a distance all this time. He was taking pictures of you to take with him. He knew how much you loved your dad and he had decided to leave town and never tell you about the affair. You and Annie are all he has. He took the teddy bear to remember the baby. Just like us, he loved her even before she was born. He never meant to scare you, honey. He was coming to tell you how sorry he was when he found you in the fire.

Jenna sat silently, trying to absorb all this new, heart-wrenching information.

"I hired a lawyer for him and he's out of jail. All the charges have been dropped. He wants to see you, but I told him not until you're ready. He's a good kid, Jen. He's hurting, too. He's had a lot of rejection in his life, but he says he'll understand if you never want to see him again."

Jenna finally cried and Tim held her. She cried for Benny, for his mom and for her parents. It was like losing them all over again. She cried for all she had lost in the fire, for the terror she felt with a knife at her throat and for almost losing little Annie. She cried for herself and Tim held her.

She was exhausted and Tim tucked her into bed, close to Annie's crib. She slept, Annie slept and Tim watched them breathe in and out.

Beverly Miller

About the Author

Beverly Miller's love of antiques and decorating, transforms a dilapidated old house into a country inn. The Inn at Willow Creek contains characters inspired by the folks she has met along life's journey.

She grew up in the heartland of America, where her life has been filled with memories and experiences that she draws from, as she writes about ordinary people doing extraordinary things.

Beverly owns a unique country store on the farm she shares with her husband in central Iowa. Her children and grandchildren all live nearby and are a constant inspiration.

She enjoys writing, nature, antique shops, art, music and spending time with family and friends.

Printed in the United States
1295100002B/72

9 781410 744227